MEETING LUCIANO

MEETING LUCIANO

a novel by

ANNA ESAKI-SMITH

ALGONQUIN BOOKS OF CHAPEL HILL
1999

Published by
ALGONQUIN BOOKS OF CHAPEL HILL
Post Office Box 2225
Chapel Hill, North Carolina 27515-2225

a division of
Workman Publishing
708 Broadway
New York, New York 10003

This is a work of fiction. While, as in all fiction, the literary perceptions and insights are based on experience, all names, characters, places, and incidents are either products of the author's imagination or are used fictitiously.

Library of Congress Cataloging-in-Publication Data
Esaki-Smith, Anna.
    Meeting Luciano : a novel / Anna Esaki-Smith.
       p.   cm.
    ISBN 1-56512-215-1
    1. Japanese Americans—Travel—Japan—Fiction.   I. Title.
    PS3555.S23 M44   1999
    813'.54—dc21   98-46878
                                                            CIP

10   9   8   7   6   5   4   3   2   1
First Edition

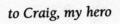
to Craig, my hero

many heartfelt thanks to:

Henry Dunow

Shannon Ravenel

Lilia Ognayon

Sun JuFang

and most of all,
my parents

O N E

There are two kinds of parents: those who bring you up with stories of their childhood, and others who act like they never had one. My mother told me everything: how her family chilled a watermelon during the summer by dropping it down a well in the morning and retrieving it at dinner, and of evenings spent in rowboats watching plankton glow in the dark. I knew she put on singing shows for her relatives, that her best friend was the daughter of the man who made her shoes, that she ate ice cream for the first time at five. Her father dropped dead from a heart attack at a train station; she loved her nurse more than her mother. My mother was filled with stories, and she'd tell them in clear, precisely chosen English, her eyes black as wet stones.

On the day I returned home from college, my mother told me about her brother.

"He was a very talented musician. A drummer." She laughed. "The girls really went for that, especially on an island where most men like to fish.

"He studied with that American, Buddy Rich," she continued. "Isn't he famous?"

I nodded, vaguely remembering a name from a television show.

My mother tapped a beat with both her index fingers on the kitchen tabletop. "But my brother's talents were not just limited to drums. He loved all music. When I was a little girl, maybe six or seven years old, he taught me this melody, which he had me sing over and over again. Even at that age I could understand the beauty of the song."

She broke out into her trembling soprano, the thin, silvery notes melting into one another like snowflakes on a fingertip. She watched me listen. Her voice strained, reaching for a particularly high note.

"You get the idea," she said, clearing her throat. "So, after I memorized the song completely, my brother sang an accompanying melody, and it became this beautiful duet. I loved being with him. We would sit outside on summer evenings and sing in the dark. Just us and our voices."

"You and Uncle Kahei? Or was that Uncle Goro?" I asked.

"Neither. His name was Kazu. He died," my mother replied.

I had never heard of Kazu. My mother was from a large family, and there had been so many deaths (a sister who committed suicide, a brother hit by a car, a half brother killed by stomach cancer) that I was never able to keep straight who had died. I was no longer surprised at being surprised by my mother's stories. There were always stories within her stories, small bombs set to explode at some disconcerting point.

"Tuberculosis," my mother added. "Everyone died of tuberculosis back then."

We sat in silence. My mother remained dry-eyed but her momentum had slowed. "Go on," I prompted, and she continued:

"Many years later, after your father and I had come to America, I went to the opera. The Metropolitan Opera Company was performing *Don Giovanni*. The sets were so impressive and the costumes were so complicated. At first, I thought the opera was just a busy spectacle. But then the characters Don Giovanni and Zerlina began singing and suddenly I was transported. They were singing our duet."

My mother began the melody again, her voice softer now. *"Vieni, mio bel diletto,"* she sang, her mouth carefully shaping the Italian. *"Io cangierò tua sorte. Andiam, andiam, mio bene, a ristorar le pene d'un innocente amor."* This time she hit all the high notes.

"It's called 'Là ci darem la mano,'" my mother informed me, after finishing. "'There we'll hold hands.' *Duettino*. That's Italian for little duet."

"I see."

My mother made a little sucking noise in her mouth, trying to extract something left over from lunch. "I've got tickets to see *L'elisir d'amore* tonight. It's a preseason benefit with Pavarotti. I'm going with Mrs. Murata."

Mrs. Murata was a college friend of my mother's who made a fortune opening a chain of take-out sushi shops in Manhattan called Sushi Yes! My mother had introduced her to the opera.

"Front-row seats," my mother continued. "So when Pavarotti spits, I'll feel it."

"That's nice," I said.

"Maybe I'll teach you my brother's part and we can sing together."

I shook my head. "You know my voice stinks," I said.

My mother nodded. "Your voice is terrible but you have perfect pitch. A duet is still possible."

"I doubt it," I replied.

MY MOTHER LEFT for the opera in the late afternoon. Whenever she went to the opera, she made an effort to dress up, digging into her crowded closet for a pocketbook and shoes that matched, spraying old, heavy perfume in her hair. Although raised in Japan during the war, she prided herself on an appreciation of the West, to the point of distancing herself from her own culture. When visiting the Metropolitan Museum of Art, she avoided the Asian wing. She never attended touring performances of kabuki or bunraku, and she criticized the limited repertoire of Japanese cuisine.

She fancied herself not American but broadly European, having worked as a secretary at the British embassy in Tokyo before getting married. She followed what she believed to be a distinctly European manner, writing careful letters when a phone call would do, saying "Pardon?" instead of "What?" Whenever she ate soup, she'd scoop the spoon away from her before lifting it silently to her mouth, taking care never to slurp the way Japanese do when eating noodles. She inevitably dribbled soup down her chin. She studied Romanesque architecture in her middle age, and more recently had grown obsessed with Italian opera. It was as though she were on a quest, moving through the geography of Western civilization in search of an essence that could finally transform her. She tried to make us as European as she possibly could, too, serving us crustless cucumber sandwiches for lunch and giving us leather satchels to take to school instead of backpacks.

Still, she fit imperfectly into this world. After dinner at a French restaurant, she'd return home and make herself a bowl of rice and miso soup. She read Japanese newspapers. The only time she seemed natural and confident was when cloaked in kimono. Tonight, as she hunted for car keys, the neckline of her dress billowed to reveal a large expanse of white skin.

After my mother left, I looked in the refrigerator for something to eat, peeling open clumps of aluminum foil and yellowed Tupperware containers, but found nothing inspiring. Growing up, I marveled at the refrigerators of my friends, gleaming iceboxes that produced platters of cold chicken and bowls of potato salad, or frosted cakes from which precisely cut slices were missing. It seemed as if attractive leftovers, wood-paneled family rooms, and golden retrievers were written into their genetic code. Our home was never so consistent. I was once humiliated when a friend opened our refrigerator door to find an octopus tentacle curled in a stainless steel bowl.

I ate leftover sukiyaki and a bowl of minestrone soup that evening, watching a rerun of *The Mary Tyler Moore Show,* and went to bed feeling sluggish.

MY LAST DAY at college had been depressing; the bars and restaurants were empty and somber. At the bagel shop, the girl behind the counter had greeted me with a yawn so big I could see clear to her tonsils. I walked slowly back to my car, hot coffee leaking out of a paper bag. Even though only a few days had passed since graduation, I felt as if I had never been there; the town had already changed, readying itself for its new occupants. I felt vaguely betrayed.

I drove out of town toward a stubbornly outdated vision of home life—a regular two-parent family, all the bedrooms filled, the house not yet worn down. I imagined the driveway perfectly sealed, the lawn mowed to an even green sheen, and the azalea shrubs trimmed into lush pink domes. The image persisted as I neared my hometown, even as the roads grew so familiar that it seemed I could drive by feel. It wasn't until I walked into the house, years of disrepair and emptiness gnawing at its soul, that I fully understood how wrong the vision was.

Late that night, as I lay under my sheet, trying with difficulty to imagine a Japanese man playing the drums, my mother's small, round shape appeared in the doorway. "Something tremendous has happened," she whispered hoarsely.

I propped myself up on my elbows. She clapped her hands.

"I met Luciano!" she exclaimed in a shrill, girlish voice.

I blinked at her. "Luciano?"

"Pavarotti. Luciano Pavarotti."

I sat up further, squinting into the light from the hallway at her silhouette. "How did you manage that?" I asked.

"Mrs. Murata donated a great deal of money to the

Westchester Arts Council. Tons of money. So we were invited backstage after the performance to meet the singers. We actually went into his dressing room." My mother laughed loudly, her voice uneven with excitement. She walked to the side of my bed, her clothes smelling of L'Air du Temps.

"Is he fat?" I asked, not knowing what else to say.

"He's not fat," my mother replied. "He's grand."

I laughed and settled back into bed.

"He was in full makeup and still dressed as Nemorino when we met him," she said. "It was like talking to some kind of god." She was silent for a moment. "Yes. Pavarotti is my god," she said, and turned and walked out of the room. The hall light switched off a second later.

G OD WAS STILL with us at breakfast the next morning. My mother kept reliving the ten minutes she had spent in his dressing room, unearthing new details about the encounter, each trip back sending her into paroxysms of happiness.

"He gets these charming lines by the corners of his eyes when he smiles," my mother said.

"They're called crow's-feet," I told her. "Everyone gets them at some point."

My mother ignored my observation. "And his complexion was lovely, the color of apricots," she continued. "I wanted to touch it. And his pores were very large."

My mother had prepared a lavish breakfast in apparent celebration of the previous evening's excitement: poached eggs with pimientos, broiled Italian sausage, sliced bread grilled with olive oil. She ate with gusto, sending particles of egg flying onto the table as she spoke.

"We had a wonderful conversation about music and operas. I'm afraid Mrs. Murata felt quite left out." My mother laughed with delight. "I told Luciano where I lived and he loves Westchester! So many trees, he said. I felt like we had so much in common. We made a connection."

She shook two spoonfuls of sugar into her coffee and drank the entire cup without stirring. When I laughed at her she giggled, rubbing her palms together while wriggling in her chair. It was as if a window had opened, flooding her with light.

OUR HOUSE WAS a builder's house, a split-level built in 1953: four bedrooms, two bathrooms, living room, dining room, and den, with an acre of wooded land separating us from our neighbors. Our street cut across a hill, with a row of houses on the high side and a row on the low. We felt lucky being on the high side, looking down on the houses across the street. From our front picture window, I could see directly into the rooms of the houses below: a family arguing over dinner, a man washing dishes without a shirt on, a black dog sleeping on a white sofa. We were too high for anyone across the street to see anything but ceilings through our windows. When I was younger, I liked to think people looking up at our pink house found it mysterious.

But, untouched for thirty years, our house had grown tired and soft. Mice ran between the walls, their feet tapping lightly as we tried to sleep. The mice never bothered my mother. She was raised in a small fishing village in Japan, a country girl accustomed to vermin and disease and death. My sister Charlotte and I, reared on a diet of television comedies and the tidy suburban homes of our friends, pleaded with her to fix the house: We were afraid of termites and flying ants; we would complain the dust was making our eyes swell and skin itch. She conceded that the house was in need of repair and that with Pappa gone she had fallen behind. Yet while her alimony checks seemed to get her comfortably through each month, nothing was ever left over. And the house remained the same, year after year.

Then, one evening, a week after my return, my mother told me about Alex.

She described him as Greek with a big truck. She said he would come the next day and begin tearing up the kitchen.

"Glory hallelujah," I said.

"He's quite charming, and very tall," she said, drinking a cup of hot water. When she told me that, my heart sank.

Charm was high on her list of desirable qualities, way above trustworthiness and normality.

My mother nodded to herself. "I have a good feeling about Alex," she said, rubbing away a faint spot on the table with her finger. "I also found a wonderful store in Darien. I'm going to pick out new cabinets, and we're going to have new floors, windows, and stovetop. I'm switching from electric to gas. Everything is going to change."

We both fell silent, each contemplating the enormity of the task. The windowpanes, painted by the night, turned pitch-black and the kitchen grew thickly quiet. The refrigerator made a tinkling noise.

My mother had told me that she would always keep the house, even after the divorce. She said it was important for people to be rooted, to feel like they had a home, not to amble through life without knowing where their hearts lie. She said the knowledge that her family house, a big, rambling wooden structure with a shiny black-tiled roof, still waited for her on a tiny Japanese island helped her get through Pappa's departure. I never understood how a house could help. Our house was too full of clutter to be of any comfort to me.

Sighing, my mother went to the stove and picked up a kettle full of boiled water.

I had always thought of my mother as a tea drinker, sitting at the kitchen table with a porcelain cup, her pointed white feet perched on a nearby seat. Tins of Japanese tea— hoji-cha, mugi-cha, and ma-cha—used to line a greasy kitchen shelf on which also sat two ceramic teapots, both older than me. One, glazed black, could steep enough for five cups, and the other, small and silvery, enough for one.

But now the tea tins were gone.

"I only have good feelings about hot water," she told me, pouring herself a cup. She brought the cup back to the table and crossed her arms low on her chest.

"When I was little," my mother said, "we would bring tin lunchboxes to school, and after we had eaten, our teacher made us pour hot water from a pot on a wood-stove into the boxes. We stirred up the rice and food stuck at the bottom with our chopsticks, and then we drank the water."

My mother acted this out for me as she spoke, using the flat of her palm as the lunchbox, the other hand holding an imaginary pair of chopsticks that she wiggled in the air. Then she pretended to drink from both palms.

"It was a smart idea," my mother said. "It kept us warm, and helped our digestion."

"That's a good one," I said.

Her eyes darted about the kitchen, from the empty cabinets above the refrigerator (too high for her to reach), to the blue bucket (filled with raw rice) in a corner on the floor.

"Let's go to bed now," she said. "We have a big day to-morrow."

I slept in my brother's old room, staring at a curling poster of the Leaning Tower of Pisa. My small room felt too much like a closet, filled with useless college papers and piles of dusty clothes. My mother slept in Charlotte's room, wearing my father's bathrobe.

I WOKE TO the sound of ripping. By the time I got downstairs, the kitchen floor was gone and the caramel-varnished wood cabinets were a pile in the garage. An old man was in the kitchen, removing nails from the wall with the claw of his hammer.

"Are you Alex?" I asked.

He extended a hand, calloused and hard as bark. "Hello there, young lady," he said with a faint accent that sounded vaguely Transylvanian to me. "You must be Emily."

"Is my mother around?" I asked.

He gestured with a jerk of his head. "She's outside. Very nice lady, your mother. Gave me a cup of hot coffee, first thing."

"You work alone?"

Alex let out a raspy laugh, revealing large white teeth. "I'm my own boss. Got the brains and I got the hands."

He held up his hands, perfectly still, for a remarkably long time. His square fingers looked as if the tips had been snipped off.

"These can do anything," he said, and winked.

I found my mother outside, dressed in sweatpants and a lightweight red windbreaker to ward off the early June chill. She roamed the backyard wildly, each stride punctuated by a poke in the ground with a stick.

"Good morning!" she exclaimed. I walked gingerly toward her, my thin bedslippers unable to absorb the rocks and twigs. "Don't you think your contractor is a bit old?" I asked.

"Oh, Alex. A charming man," my mother said, and inhaled deeply. "He says he can finish the kitchen in a week. We won't be able to use the stove, so I thought we would hibachi outside. Won't that be fun? We haven't hibachied in such a long time."

She peered into space, as if trying to count the pollen in the air. Her profile revealed a slight underbite. Against the many straight elms dotting the yard, she looked shrunken, like an elf who had sprung from the trunk of a tree.

"I have to go to the steakhouse later today," I told her. "Are you going to be O.K. by yourself?"

Smiling, she closed her eyes and nodded without looking at me. "Sure. Everything's just fine."

Through the kitchen window, I saw the flash of a hammer as Alex banged at the wall. The house's pink shingles were tinged with brown. Moss crawled over the slate walkway. My mother stood on top of the hill, resting her hand on the stick, and surveyed her overgrown yard like a kingdom.

THE RENOVATION WILL proceed as follows, my mother explained: (A) Get the kitchen done: It is the engine of our house and must be repaired first; (B) Fix everything else.

"This might take some time," I said.

Later that afternoon, Alex took down the kitchen door while my mother cleaned the refrigerator. She pulled out a container of yogurt, checked the bottom for an expiration date, and threw it in the garbage. Alex hummed like a bee. "Bzzz, bzzz, bzzz," he droned as his screwdriver skipped over a stubborn hinge. His hair was very white, weighted with dust and slightly yellowed at the ends as if dipped in honey.

"If you don't mind me saying, this house is not in good shape," Alex said, shaking his head.

My mother examined a carton of milk. "I haven't lived in this house for many years," she murmured.

Alex raised his bushy eyebrows. "You've been away?"

"No, no, no. I mean spiritually. I haven't lived here in my mind."

Alex was silent a moment, and then resumed working away at the hinge.

SADO WAS AN island not worth bombing during the war. It floats just west of mainland Japan, a tiny rivet of red earth and trees, surrounded by fishing boats bobbing in a steely sea. Even my mother, born and raised there, needs a few moments to find it on the map.

Life on Sado during the war wasn't much different from life there at any other time. The sugar, from Taiwan, and the toilet paper, from Manchuria, were rationed, and families ate ground eggshells for calcium, but other than that, things stayed pretty much the same. The sea held plenty of squid and snapper, vegetables grew in everyone's backyard, and the fields were thick with rice. Nobody outside Sado wanted anything the island had to offer. The war, just a three-hour ferry ride away, was part of another world.

This disappointed me. In the war I imagined, shells exploded around my parents as they clung to one another— two young people escaping to the protective solitude of a temple tended by a quiet monk, falling in love. But Sado remained as still then, my mother said, as it had been a thousand years before. "And as much as I wanted to kill myself when he left me," she said once, "your father and I were never in love."

My mother was the youngest daughter of the richest family on the island. They managed most of the rice fields, ran a sake brewery, lived in two large wooden houses, and owned a mountain inhabited by monkeys. When she was little, she'd stand on a table and sing and dance while her friends stood gathered around her on the floor. In photos taken at that time, her wide face looks confident and bored, nearly sullen, an indulged girl. Some of these pictures were stored in a cardboard shoebox on a bookshelf in our living room. It was a modest collection of sepia-toned images peopled with small, thin figures, their sharp, angular features as precisely drawn and delicate as the faces on dolls. And like dried bits of paper that bloomed into flowers when submerged in water, my mother would unfold these concentrated pieces of the past into elaborate stories.

"*Mio dio!*" my mother said, sitting by the bookcase. With the entire house a mess, she had decided to sort pictures. This was how she did things: Facing a huge task, she always focused on the minute, as if the rest of her life were already in perfect working order.

Turning a photo toward me, she pointed a finger to a young girl's face.

"This looks like you," she told me.

"You think I look like that? Charlotte resembles you more," I replied.

My mother examined the photo closely, holding it near her face to deflect the light from the window. "This was taken during a particularly wonderful time. My mother invited sumo wrestlers to the house for the entire summer."

I sat on the floor beside her, ungainly and inelegant by comparison, my legs unable to lie flat in any direction. My mother sat in a neat, tight package, her legs tucked beneath her. In the photo, she is about ten years old and stands between two bulky men, both dressed in light cotton yukata and wooden sandals, their oiled hair folded into topknots on their heads.

"What did they do all summer?" I asked.

"Sleep. And eat, of course. They were actually quite charming. Luckily, we had a bathtub big enough for them to fit into. That was truly a luxury for them. And, much to my surprise, they bathed quite cleanly."

I laughed. "You mean often?"

My mother shook her head, inserting the photo back into the shoebox. "No, not at all. I mean cleanly. Our servants would draw up only one bath a day, then they would heat the water by setting a wood fire under the tub, and keep it going by blowing through a long bamboo tube. It was a difficult task." She flicked through a few more pictures: a school photo, family portrait, wedding. "Then we'd take turns bathing, sometimes five people or more would use the water in one day. So it was important that you washed all the dirt on your body before you entered the tub. And after you soaked, it was polite to make sure nothing was floating in the water, like a piece of hair. Anyway, we were concerned about the wrestlers, but they were very clean bathers."

"Sounds disgusting," I said. I found it difficult to believe that huge, fleshy men, encumbered by massive rolls of fat and skin, could be so meticulous.

"Really? I always thought it gave bathing a nice family feeling. Anyway, since I was the littlest, I always went last. I could be as dirty as I wanted."

She sighed, brushing a speck of dust from the photo with her finger. "It's strange to think how little you know about life at any time. If someone were to have told me when I was ten that I'd end up alone in America, it would have seemed crazy. But here I am."

She began slipping the pictures into a photo album, her moves swift and efficient, and then brought the album upstairs to her room. Gentleness had surrounded her in those early years, not only through the kindness of her nanny and the villagers, but from Sado itself: the rolling slopes of its lush, green hills, the tender white fish eaten every day, the lazy curl of smoke rising from her nightly mosquito coil. Life had been a safe, sleepy journey for my mother, and there was no reason then for her not to expect that it would continue to be so.

HOMES ARE LIKE masks. My mother thought that people who lived in big houses had different lives, that, because of the beautiful decor, somehow the fabric of their lives was more richly embroidered. I think she imagined faint music playing all the time in these homes, like a soundtrack in a movie, even while people sat in them alone. When the leaves dropped in late autumn, she'd pile us in the car with a basket of panini sandwiches and cruise the back roads of Greenwich or Bedford, slowing down when passing a particularly stately home. She'd peer into windows, even creep down private roads, to our collective horror, turning around on raked gravel driveways, the crunching of our tires threatening to give us away. There were a few spectacular houses that we'd pass regularly, even though we could only snatch glimpses of stone or brick beyond gates and strategically placed evergreens. My mother knew the names of many of the families in these homes. "The Firestones live there," she'd tell us, or, "That's the DuPont house."

She'd hold these rich families up as models for us, and I thought for a while that she had some actual knowledge about the personal lives of these families. Then, on my first summer back from college, I was invited by a friend into one of these homes. My mother was more excited than I and dropped me off at the front door. But, inside, I found a window-wrapped family room filled with a television's flickering blue and orange light. My friend's parents were watching *Lifestyles of the Rich and Famous*. The elegant features of the room made its human occupants seem pathetic in their ordinariness, the house somehow dishonest.

THE LAST OWNER of our house killed himself. Mr. Cortez had moved his wife and small daughter in, had created a home life for three years and then hanged himself in the backyard. The light fixture in our front hallway was his: a glass cylinder enclosing three flame-shaped bulbs, each bulb burning out in turn, never together. As a child,

I wondered if his daughter thought of those three bulbs as her family. For a while, I assigned a bulb to me, the two others to Charlotte and my little brother, Pierre, and would wait to see which one burned out first.

My mother gave Alex careful instructions not to touch the light. He was still busy with the kitchen, but she wanted him to know. It was as if for her, too, the light had some special meaning. I had never asked her about it, and never told her what it had meant to me.

My mother stood on a stepladder with a rag in her hand, delicately dusting between the plastic candles and wiping the bulbs. Even when balanced on the top step, she could barely reach the light.

"You hungry?" she asked. I was sitting in the living room between dishes stacked on the couch. The coffee table and love seat were loaded with bottles of soy sauce and extra-virgin olive oil, containers of instant fish broth, packages of dried rice noodles, packets of whole wheat, egg, and spinach pasta, dried seaweed, sun-dried tomatoes, dried shiitake and porcini mushrooms. It was as if my mother had been stocking up for a nuclear war. In the kitchen, the sink was gone. The stove and refrigerator were disconnected.

"We can't make anything," I said.

"We can always make something," my mother said in her folkloric way.

• • •

A FISH LAY in the garage. Still whole, its bruised eye peeking out from behind newspaper, it was firm and cool. Before lighting the hibachi in the backyard, my mother briskly rubbed her hands together. She was good with coals. She used a paper fan, coaxing them to orange, and put the fish on the grill when ash appeared.

Back inside the living room, she plugged in the rice cooker next to the stereo. Meanwhile, Alex stripped the wallpaper in the kitchen. Bright yellow flowers had covered the kitchen walls ever since I was six. Now, even after the paper was removed, the pattern's ghost remained, as if burned onto the plaster by a photographic flash. Alex tore down the paper panels with relish, crumpling each into a ball, which he tossed in a corner.

He watched me bring the blackened, crusty fish to the table as my mother sliced cucumbers that had been packed overnight in vinegar and salt. The three of us ate in the torn-up kitchen, my mother and I at the Formica table, Alex with his sandwich, leaning against the far wall.

"You always eat like that?" he asked, his mouth full of salami.

"Oh no," my mother replied. "This is just simple food."

The fish was perfectly cleaned and had been soaked in soy sauce, wine, and ginger. The cucumbers tasted salty and sweet at the same time. I was intimately familiar with this food, and although I couldn't imagine my life without it, I felt as if I could never make it properly myself.

Alex shook his head. "That doesn't look so simple to me."

My mother laughed. "You have no idea! You should have seen the complicated food I have made in this kitchen. Let's see, what might have been the most fantastic—"

"The *supplì al telefono*," I offered. "That was pretty complicated."

"Oh, yes. *Supplì al telefono*. You deep-fry rice balls in each of which a cube of mozzarella cheese has been inserted. When you pull the cooked *supplì* apart, the mozzarella has melted and is stretched into strings, like telephone wires. Delicious.

"This," my mother said, almost apologetically, gesturing to the fish, "is food I was brought up on. I find that as I get older, I go back to my childhood."

"I agree, I agree," said Alex, becoming animated as he wiped a hand on his thigh. "When I was growing up, my mother knew how to make spanakopita and stuffed grape leaves better than anyone. Trouble is that now no one in my family knows how to make food anymore. Real food. What I would give to eat something of my mother's now instead of this." He looked at his sandwich as if expecting it to speak.

"You should learn from your mother," Alex told me, taking another bite.

I thought of her rinsing vegetables in ice-cold water,

cutting tofu into cubes on her palm, flattening meat with her fist—simple things I had never done. My mother was also adept at the uncommon: packing salmon in the fermented rice mash left over from brewing sake; cooking ceremonial sticky rice dotted with red beans; stewing squid with boiled, grated radish. Learning her cooking was always something I had thought would come easier the closer I got to being an adult. Now, I realized, it would require becoming a different person.

"There is no reason to teach her," my mother said, retrieving a stray grain of rice from her lip with a finger. "You're not going to marry people who eat this food. I don't want you living with one foot here and the other in Japan."

She spoke evenly, picking hair-thin bones out of the fish with her chopsticks.

MY MOTHER HAD had plans for Charlotte and me: We would go to college and meet and marry well-bred men with good teeth who would connect us to America's gleaming mainstream. But none of those men ever asked me out. During my freshman year, I had dates with a Chinese exchange student who approached me because he thought I was also Chinese; then a handsome alcoholic senior who beerily professed love of all things Oriental on our second, and last, date; and finally an electrical engineering major who twitched as if being taunted with a cattle prod. Things didn't get much better my sophomore year. "This is all your father's fault," my mother would say over the phone. "He has damaged something in your mind." I didn't take her comment that seriously. But women all around me seemed to find boyfriends effortlessly and I started feeling very alone among the airy Frisbee-playing sylphs on the arts quad. At night, I walked home through campus quickly, avoiding big pockets of darkness.

Friday nights often cornered me in the library, where I would retreat from my dormitory's raucous anticipation of the weekend. Or I would sit for hours at my drawing table in the studio, but do little more than stare out the window. Laughter and the occasional whoop echoed from the street below.

On Saturday nights, I did my laundry. Laundry became an obsession. I'd divide my clothes not only into darks and lights, but into nuanced subdivisions of the two. I mixed complex concoctions of detergents to get just the right scent. I knew exactly when to pour in the softener or color-safe bleach. I spray-starched my sheets, pillowcases, and the collars of all my shirts; I folded my clean under-wear and bras into little rosettes.

One night, as I descended into the familiar basement, a boy was there, sitting on top of a washer, reading a book. His tangled blond hair hung to his shoulders like an over-grown plant. He had one load going through the rinse cycle, another tumbling in the dryer.

I was slightly annoyed. It had taken a long time to get accustomed to spending Saturday nights alone, and I had grown to enjoy my solitary routine.

When I deposited my red plastic laundry basket on a washer with a little thump, the boy's head flew up. He turned to me, his dilated eyes like ink.

I began grouping my clothes into their many categories and was relieved to hear his washer whine into what I hoped was its final spin. A few minutes later the machine clicked off and the boy slipped down from his perch. I looked up to see him pulling a long, dark vine of clothes out of the washer. If I actually liked it down here with all my soaps and softeners, I thought, maybe my mother was right. Maybe there was something wrong with me.

"It's nice doing laundry at night, isn't it?" the boy said suddenly.

"Huh?" I responded as I pulled from my basket a long, black sock.

"The way the air smells, the way clothes feel when they're wet. It's nice."

He spoke clearly and directly, as if he were addressing a class while facing a blackboard. Then he turned to me, expectant.

"I never really thought about it," I replied, but laughed because, in fact, I agreed.

"I've seen you on campus before," the boy said. He

stuffed his wet clothes into another dryer and slammed the lid closed.

"You were with an architecture class, sitting on the grass, sketching one of the buildings," the boy said, walking toward me. He stopped three Whirlpools away from where I stood. As he leaned up against the machine, I noted he was short, his waist not quite meeting the lid. "I saw your drawing, which I thought was quite good."

"Thanks," I said.

We were both quiet, the rhythmic tumbling of clothes in the dryer keeping time like a metronome. The rivets on a pair of his jeans pinged irregularly. The dryer is me, I thought, regular, predictable. He's freer, spontaneous, like the pinging.

"I'm Ben," the boy said.

"Hi," I said. I raised my eyebrows as if I had something bright to say, but could think of nothing.

I resumed picking out my dark clothes, listlessly depositing them into a pile on the folding table. The jeans kept going around the dryer; *ping, pingping*.

"Want to go for coffee?" Ben asked.

MY PARENTS CAME to America in 1964, first spending a week in Honolulu. I have seen photos of them with thick leis around their necks, always standing apart as if making room for someone in between. Their next stop was New York. My mother ate a plate of cottage cheese at the Kennedy airport cafeteria, thinking it was chopped tofu. "So sour," she would later say, making a puckered face.

When they moved to Pleasant Springs, the neighbors thought they were Mexican. "Olé, olé!" kids would yell as they rode by on bikes. Japan was on the other side of the earth, and there didn't seem to be any reason for people to travel so far.

And then my father left. His decision to leave us came suddenly when I was nineteen. He didn't announce his intention to me directly, but my mother kept me up late one night to tell me he would be gone at any moment. She knew many of his reasons.

"Mom says you're having an affair with someone," I told my father the next day. He was sitting in his smoky den, the white walls long turned to gray. I stood by the door. "That's why you want a divorce."

"Not true," he said.

"So she's lying to me?"

Pappa rubbed his eyes. His legs were crossed, and a beaten leather slipper hung from the toes of his left foot.

"She's turned you against me, Emily. My reasons are very complicated."

He spoke with a conviction equal to my mother's, although his words were measured and drained. My mother was more dramatic, gesturing with her white arms. Her comforting coolness changed into a confined kind of resentment, like an alert, active animal kept in a closed box. She snipped photos of my father into sharp pieces and sprinkled them on top of the garbage.

Pappa left one night while I was sleeping. When I awoke, I didn't know anything had happened until I noticed that his shoes, which my mother kept lined up by the hall closet, were gone. The rest of the house seemed normal. The dishwasher was on. My mother was sitting in the kitchen in her bathrobe, with a cup of tea cooling on the table. She had taken her slippers off, and her feet were propped up on my father's chair. I walked into the room gingerly, afraid of making noise.

"Is he gone?" I asked.

My mother nodded. "Breakfast?" she said.

Now, I no longer understood the dynamics of the house; the television seemed too far away from the sofa, the doorbell sounded too loud, my mattress felt too hard. Yet, after four years away, I couldn't accurately remember what it was like before. My father, sister, and brother had left behind most of their belongings, as if they had fled during some emergency. Perhaps it was the absence of their bodies that skewed the dimensions and the acoustics of the house I had known.

Charlotte called in the early afternoon, a food processor grinding over the phone.

"I'm making a cold soup," she said, her voice close to

my ear, as if her lips were pressed against the receiver. She paused a second after something clattered to the ground. "Gazpacho," she added.

The food processor began whirring in fits and starts. "I'm 'pulsing,'" Charlotte informed me. "So how's the house?"

"You know about the renovation?"

"Sure. Mom called me early this morning. Really early. I haven't heard her so excited about anything in a long time."

"She has been acting a little strangely."

"How so?"

"I haven't figured it out yet exactly." I watched her from my brother's bedroom window, chatting up Alex in the driveway. "She's got this contractor here tearing things up left and right, and she strolls around the mess like a monk. This morning there were a few rocks in a pile in the back-yard, and she told me they suggested a crane."

Charlotte laughed. "She'll probably start throwing salt around the kitchen in some kind of purification rite."

We often joked about our family and the odd inner logic our parents had developed, like eating lasagna at Thanksgiving or taking our shoes off at the front door even though the floors left our socks blackened. But we never questioned our private customs and followed the rit-uals with the same matter-of-factness as other families on our street, who roasted turkeys for holidays and went to church on Sundays.

I asked how she was doing.

"Chicago's great, my apartment's great, the kitchen's got all this counter space," she said. "When are you coming to visit?"

I fingered one of Pierre's high school soccer trophies. "Soon, when Mom gets the house business straightened out," I replied.

"Hey, she told me about meeting Pavarotti, too. That's pretty amazing."

"I think she wants to bear his children."

Charlotte pulsed her gazpacho some more and talked about her job at the bank before we hung up. I always used my sister as a gauge for what was normal and abnormal in this world. For as long as I could remember, our family had lived a ramshackle life. My parents tended to details that gradually knit together into something bigger rather than dividing life into a series of categories, like work, hobbies, and health. They created a thriving chaos that in the end, to them, made sense.

But something was always left hanging, a loose end flying in the air. My mother's insistence on keeping everything, whether it be ratty rubber bands, used pieces of plastic wrap, or empty mayonnaise jars, maddened my sister.

"We're not poor!" Charlotte would say.

Harmless activities became quests. At one point, my father transformed an interest in bowling into a full-blown lifestyle. He wore bowling shirts at home and watched somber tournaments on TV. We bowled every Thursday and Saturday evening for five straight months (with none of us quite able to understand the scoring). My mother complained the entire time that bowling was a crude American version of bocci ball. And it ended when she bought a bocci set that is still in our garage. We never used it because our yard was too sloped.

But my sister was the most well-adjusted person I knew, exercising regularly, flossing her teeth, taking her red Toyota in for oil changes every three months. It was as if having triumphed over overwhelming idiosyncrasy she reveled in routine, in being like everyone else and nothing like our parents.

My mother knocked at the door. "Charlotte is fine?" she asked, leaning her head into the room. She was looking very good, a healthy pink tinting her cheeks. Her hair had been combed into a smooth cap.

"Seems that way," I replied.

"Has she found a boyfriend?" she asked, coming in.

"Not that I know of."

My mother sighed. "She should get a boyfriend. She's getting old, already twenty-nine. You should get one, too."

"Get one yourself," I said, irritated.

My brother's room felt small with both of us there, me sitting at his desk by the window, my mother standing by the bed. A boy-smell lingered in the air: baseball mitts, worn shoes, loose change.

My mother blinked rapidly and took a step toward me. "You have an extremely bad attitude."

"Me?" I replied, my voice tightening, bracing myself for the inevitable onslaught. "Getting a boyfriend isn't like shopping for a steak. Maybe that's the way it is in Japan, but I think Charlotte and I want something better."

"Better?"

My mother paused, then hit her thigh. When emotional, she made noises with her hands, clapping them at good news, softly slapping the side of her face when dismayed.

"Can't you see how alone we are? Pappa's gone, Charlotte in Chicago, Pierre in Milan. We're all like islands now." She crossed her arms tightly over her stomach. "A boyfriend can give us family and relatives, make us part of something. So for heaven's sake, don't be stupid."

THAT FIRST EVENING with Ben was a typical Saturday night in town. Bars were packed, cigarette smoke filling the spaces bodies did not. The sidewalks were soured by beer, and the streets echoed with the occasional howl of a drunken student or the sudden booming bass of a dance tune as a bar door swung open in the distant darkness.

Ben walked quickly, his trench coat flapping around him like a flag. At one point, he stopped in front of an old maple and exclaimed, "What a beautiful tree!" Though embarrassed by his undisguised effort to impress me, I stepped back a few paces and took in the tree I had passed dozens of times before. I saw that it was perfect in its symmetry, as if someone had cut its silhouette from a folded piece of paper. Its green leaves were as glossy as glass, each one quivering in the breeze like a butterfly's wing.

He led me to the front of a tiny coffee shop, opened the door, and let himself in first. "This is the best café in town," he said.

The room was small and bare, with a few posters of Ho Chi Minh City on the walls and white candles flickering on the tiny tables. Ben removed his coat with a flourish before sliding into a seat, his dramatic movements nearly blowing out the candle in front of him.

My knees bumped his as I sat down across from him. I couldn't decide which of his eyes to focus on, so I shifted from one to the other, hoping my wavering would fuse into a steady gaze.

"Something wrong with your contacts?" he asked.

"No, no," I replied, rubbing my eyes. "I'm just tired."

"Yeah, I have friends who are architecture students. For them, sleeping is just a hobby."

He leaned back in his chair and called to a waitress. "Two coffees?" He turned to me and smiled conspiratorially. "Do you know where the Vietnamese find really good coffee?"

"Where?"

"In fox shit."

"In what?"

"Vietnamese foxes eat coffee beans and expel them whole. People retrieve their shit because the foxes know how to pick the best beans. Something in their digestive system adds flavor. Coffee farmers keep their own fox coffee stash."

I laughed. "That can't be true."

"It's true. I've had it, it's great. The guy who owns this place has some. God, I'd love to go to Vietnam."

He paused for a moment, gazing at the candle that was now a pool of clear wax in a small tin base. "I'd start at Ho Chi Minh City, and stay at the Continental Hotel, where Graham Greene wrote *The Quiet American*. Then, I'd go north by train, stopping at Hue, Vietnam's Kyoto. I'd end up at Halong Bay, where the water is emerald green."

He sounded enthusiastic, but practiced. I wondered how many women had occupied my chair while he wheeled out this exotic itinerary.

"Of course, I'd go to Hanoi."

"Now's a good time to go. You'll still be able to see the city's Old Quarter before it's torn down," I said, breaking his monologue. "The buildings are French colonial—high ceilings, deep verandahs, buttressed eaves."

"Is that right? Of course, you'd know."

He laughed as the waitress set down two coffee cups between us. On top of each was a tin drip filter loaded with dark grounds.

"It's not from a fox, is it?" I asked, smiling.

Ben removed his filter and stirred up the sweet, condensed milk from the bottom of his cup with a spoon. "Unfortunately, no," he replied, and nodded toward my cup for me to do the same.

T W O

The steakhouse was a wooden farmhouse originally set near a rice field in Hokkaido. Sometime in the early 1970s, it had been transported piece by piece to a grassy spot overlooking the Saw Mill River Parkway thirty minutes north of New York City, then meticulously reconstructed, using hemp cords and strategic grooves. There wasn't a nail in the place. The menus solemnly apprised guests of the building's features, drawing their attention to the steeply slanted roof, meant to deflect snow like an Alpine chalet. The design was supposedly modeled after two hands in prayer. The joke among the chefs was that the roof was praying the farmhouse wouldn't fall down.

I had worked at the steakhouse every summer since I was fifteen, waiting tables and serving drinks festooned with pineapple slices and paper umbrellas. Within the subdued Westchester countryside, the steakhouse was known as a family restaurant, or a good dark place for high school kids to take a first date. On Friday and Saturday nights, the chefs made supreme efforts to outdo one another: tossing zucchinis in the air and catching them on their knives or spinning ceramic plates on the table like a stunt from *The Ed Sullivan Show*. Yet, despite the theatrics, there was a melancholy feeling to the steakhouse, as if, like members of a traveling circus, we had all ended up there after failing to fit in elsewhere.

During the week, when only a few diners trickled in, the slow pace sapped everyone. On those nights, the dim lighting barely hid the restaurant's shabby details: the patina of grease coating the walls, our faded cotton kimonos, the chefs' tired faces.

"Yo," Hiro called out as I walked into the kitchen. He wore a tall yellow chef's cap, slightly stained around the rim, and his mustache drooped to the corners of his mouth. He was a short, compact man with large forearms developed from years of theatrical cooking. Hiro and the other chefs were clustered around a large metal table, picking through piles of bean sprouts and cleaning vegetables.

"How's business?" I asked.

"Business is good," Hiro said, peeling an onion with quick jerks of his knife.

"Anybody famous come by recently?"

Hiro paused, staring at the greenish-white ball in his hand as if peering into the past. "Simon, but without Garfunkel," he said. "Sam Donaldson, who was wearing a thick toupee. And Peter Frampton. But he only ordered vegetables. I asked him, 'If you want vegetables, why did you come to a steakhouse?' Stupid."

Hiro was friendly, and, for a Japanese, unusually cynical. From the first day I met him, he treated me like an equal, while the other chefs viewed the waitresses as useful but mostly decorative.

A busboy burst in the swinging kitchen door, bringing with him the smell of grease from the dining room. I breathed it in and felt deeply depressed. During my summer stints, I liked knowing I would be there only for a few months, that by the end of August I could leave my kimono behind. Now I didn't know how long I'd have to wear the thing.

"We're offering crab legs now," Hiro added. "You should watch us crack those legs."

He unsheathed a knife from the holster on his belt and, holding the handle with both hands, lifted it in the air, samurai-style.

"We get good tips," he added, bringing the knife down in slow motion, then sliding it back into his belt.

I examined the cartons of ice cream packed into the freezer. "Cherry pistachio's new too," I said.

"Yes. Disgusting, but popular," Hiro replied. The other chefs mumbled in agreement.

"How's Mariko?" I asked.

"Mariko is Mariko," he said, stripping another onion of its brittle brown skin.

I went downstairs to the ladies' locker room. My two-piece kimono was where I had left it the year before, the cotton top and bottom neatly folded in a cubbyhole, the heavy embroidered sash curled on top like a sleeping cat. I held the kimono to my nose, breathing in the scent of laundry soap still laced with the smell of grilled meat. The oily smoke from the open grills never washed out. Mariko had set aside a fresh pair of tabi for me, ironed and rolled like a wad of dollar bills. I loved the velvety tabi, fitting my feet like snug white gloves, separating my big toe from the rest.

PUTTING ON THE steakhouse kimono involved none of the silk cords and hidden ties of a real one. There was no ritualistic order to the undergarments; in fact, no undergarments were needed at all other than my own Hanes underwear. The kimono had been reduced to its barest essence. The stiff back bow of my obi sash snapped on like a little boy's necktie. My zori slippers were plastic. Changing was as simple as getting into gym clothes.

But when I looked in the full-length mirror, the illusion was startling. With my hair neatly tied back in a bun, and

my hands clasped primly in front, I could be a girl dressed
for a street festival in Tokyo. I walked around the locker
room with tiny, abbreviated steps, like I had seen my
mother do when dressed in her formal kimono, slightly
pigeon-toed to accentuate her demureness, and smiled at
how unnatural it felt.

As I sat down to adjust my top, I felt as if I had never
left the restaurant. College was already beginning to feel
like a hazy dream. I had started with a major in architecture, inspired by my mother's interests at that time and
encouraged by fine arts teachers starved for students interested in something other than business or law. But the
summer after my father left, I became compulsive about
saving money. My mother grew quiet and withdrawn, so I
compensated by busying myself with economy, turning off
lights whenever they weren't needed, snipping coupons
from newspapers, and cutting my own hair.

Although our life before was never extravagant, I was
obsessed with trimming whatever excess I could, as if
every cent I saved was helping us inch back to the way we
were before.

As my father cut off our credit cards and froze my
mother's bank accounts, all my mother could do was rant
about how his friends had betrayed her, how his company
should fire him. And I felt, for the first time, that my
mother couldn't protect me. She seemed out of reach,
adrift on her own.

"Hey, Emily! Didn't expect to see you here."

Tomoe, a half-Japanese woman in her late twenties, hauled a heavy backpack onto the bench. She smiled, her golden-brown eyes narrowing slightly.

"Well, for better or worse, I'm back," I said, sighing.

"This year's my seventh here. Can you believe it?" Tomoe slipped her clogs off and wriggled out of tight jeans. "I keep telling myself, I'm going to do something new, I'm going to try something different, but I keep coming back. I could just shoot myself."

Tomoe was beautiful, smart, and could speak smoothly fluent Japanese; it seemed it would be easy for her to do whatever she wanted. But as we dressed quietly in the locker room, it occurred to me that her reasons for being here were likely as personal and complicated as my own. She could never guess that I came back because the gaping hole my father left in my mother's life was one I had tried frantically to fill. When I returned to campus the fall after Pappa left, I switched my major to accounting, and spent the remainder of my college years in quiet agony, calculator in hand. By the time I graduated, the last thing I wanted to become was an accountant.

In the hallway, the time clock ticked like a bomb. I found my card lined up with those of the other waitresses: Mariko from Kyushu, Sachiko from Osaka, Futaba from Kobe. They were all good, hardworking people who laughed about the oppressive social rules of Japan yet hadn't found a place abroad where they wanted to stay. They had come to America, but still seemed to be searching, wandering further and further from their homes. The steakhouse, with its tropical drinks and green-tea ice cream, seemed to be only a stop on so many individual journeys.

I punched in: 4:58 P.M., two minutes early. Before heading upstairs, I paused in the empty hallway and listened to the distant clatter from the kitchen, breathing in the odor of hot soy sauce and fried meat. All those miles I had logged walking from class to class on a wide, grassy campus, the books I had bought and read, the facts and equations I had memorized in numbingly quiet libraries—all seemed to dissolve into that smell lingering in the air. I felt that no matter where I fled—to places scented with curry or basil or lemongrass—I'd still wind up here, smelling that smell.

MARIKO WAS IN the pantry preparing salads, her thick brown hands fluttering like sparrows over the bowls. She was a plump woman, in her early forties, neatly packed into a sea-gray kimono. Her cheeks dimpled whenever she moved her mouth. Hiro and Mariko were the senior statesmen of the steakhouse, each having worked there for more than a decade, but while Hiro's experience made him bored and jaded, Mariko retained the professional seriousness befitting a nun.

I walked to her side and began topping each salad bowl with three tomato wedges and three red onion rings. It was always three of each, never four, she would say. *Four,* in Japanese, was a homonym for *death.* Mariko tucked her short, wiry hair behind her ears and put her hand on my shoulder.

"Gil's dead," she said.

"Oh my God. What happened?"

Mariko shook her head solemnly. "Car crash," she replied.

Gil was everyone's favorite at the steakhouse. He was barely in his twenties, originally from the streets of gritty Osaka, and his only apparent goal in life was to own a Harley-Davidson motorcycle. At work, he wore cowboy boots with metal-tipped toes. His English was irregular and slangy. "Dudes! We're gonna chop some steak bitchin' all right!" he'd say to fellow chefs. Mariko's face remained composed, as if we were discussing the weather, but I knew Gil had been like a little brother to her. And he had always been open about his affection for her, giving her hugs or winking at her, making Hiro and the others un-comfortable.

"Fate is strange, don't you think?" Mariko asked, peel-ing away the shriveled outer leaves of a lettuce head. "Why Gil? He never asked for much. It wasn't like his desires were evil or extravagant."

"All he wanted was that motorbike."

"Yes. At least that's what he'd say. But perhaps what he really enjoyed was the idea of wanting something. It gave him a purpose. If he actually had bought the Harley, I wonder what he would have done."

Mariko said the chefs had devised a new trick in honor of Gil—dousing shrimp with cheap sherry then setting them afire. I overheard Hiro telling a customer it was called "Fire of the Orient." I followed Mariko back to the kitchen, carrying a tray of salads. Taped koto music twanged softly in my ears. The chefs wore the same colored hats as last year, with matching kerchiefs tied around their necks. The new one, Tetsu, was so thin that his belt, weighted by holstered knives, threatened to shimmy down his hips to the floor.

"I get nervous out there," he confessed as he prepared his cart, loading it with raw onion, zucchini, and steak. "So many things can go wrong."

"Just don't think about it," Hiro advised, tapping the metal tabletop with the blunt edges of two knives.

Mariko pointed to bandages wrapped around two of Hiro's fingers.

Hiro snickered. "Par for the course, stupid."

"You're the stupid one," Mariko replied.

"You are more stupid."

I slid back into the old routine, hustling bowls of salad and rice out of the kitchen, brewing thin, bitter tea for eight people at a time. I wrapped rubber bands around my kimono sleeves and pulled them up over my elbows before scooping cherry pistachio from the freezer. My tips were good.

At about nine o'clock, things began to wind down, and I went into the dining room to watch Tetsu and Hiro at their grills. They greeted guests with practiced smiles. Tetsu was obviously skilled, preparing the meat and vegetables quickly and carefully, never missing a plate when sliding the food off his knife. But Hiro put on a show. While stir-frying the zucchini, he did a frantic tap dance on the carpeted floor. He yodeled to Mariko for rice. After whistling to get Tetsu's attention, he threw a salt shaker like a football, which Tetsu had to stretch to catch. When Hiro performed "Fire of the Orient," he poured sherry recklessly, then set the entire grill aflame.

AT FIRST, MY mother's kitchen changed rapidly. Alex's renovation schedule was propelled by great bursts of energy. He'd ring our doorbell at seven in the morning, and leave only after we'd finished dinner. His enthusiasm exhausted us to the point that my mother left the garage door open overnight so he could come in the next day unannounced. He painted the walls a luminous mint green in a matter of hours, and promptly replaced our bare light bulb with a Tiffany-style stained-glass lamp similar to one my mother had seen in a magazine. He installed new floor-to-ceiling windows in two days, opening up the normally dim room to the acre of grass and birch trees in our back-yard. "Sometimes I'm so good I scare myself," he said to me through an open window, smiling as he smoked a cigarette down to his fingers outside.

I grew accustomed to having him around the house, lis-tening to his deep voice and heavy footsteps contrast with my mother's light, airy presence.

But progress began to ebb. After putting in the new cup-boards, Alex discovered that the doors were an inch too narrow, leaving a gap even when closed. He silently re-moved them. One morning, he inserted a melon rind into the new food disposal in the sink, and the grinding was so loud I could hear it through my shower upstairs. He blocked up light sockets with paint and misaligned tiles. Yet every day he presented the same ebullient optimism, as if everything was proceeding exactly as he had planned.

"I think that's mine, the mu shu pork," said Alex, point-ing to the aluminum container my mother pulled out from the bag. She passed it to him, and he opened the cardboard lid, releasing salty steam into the air.

"I can smell mu shu pork a mile away," he added brightly, peering at the dark, soy-drenched food. "I hope they didn't forget the pancakes to roll this stuff up with. It's no fun without the pancakes," he added.

"They're right here," my mother said, handing over a waxed paper bag of small, thin wheat-flour crepes. She paused, tossing packets of duck sauce and mustard onto the table. "Isn't it amazing how many countries wrap up food with pancakes? The Mexicans eat tacos. The French wrap everything in crepes—"

"And don't forget the Turks and their kebabs," Alex said. "Roast lamb in a pancake."

"The Turks wrap kebabs?" I asked, trying to catch Alex's eye. "That sounds kind of strange."

Alex nodded his head. "They definitely do," he said, although without much conviction.

"Well, I am surprised at how wonderful this food seems," my mother said, cracking apart her wooden chopsticks and shoveling a pile of white steamed rice from a paper box onto her plate. "I am pleasantly surprised."

"I thought you vowed never to buy from that restaurant. I thought you wanted them to go out of business," I said.

Alex neatly arranged a line of mu shu pork onto a pancake, dribbled on duck sauce, and rolled it into a tight cigar. "Why's that?" he asked, biting off the end.

"She thinks Chinese takeout is corrupting," I told him.

My mother, chewing a mouthful of rice, shot me a look. "No. I never said that."

I continued, ignoring her gaze. "You said a Chinese restaurant doesn't fit in a town like this. You said it takes away the town's dignity."

"Really? It seems like a decent place to me," Alex said, rolling up another pancake. "They gave me a bowl of those deep-fried noodles while I was waiting."

"What changed your mind?" I asked my mother, cracking open a fortune cookie and pulling out the strip of paper. "Problems are often unique opportunities in disguise," the fortune read.

"I simply felt like Chinese food today," she replied. "Nothing more."

"Could it be you're tired of takeout from the diner?" I asked.

My mother shook her head. "Oh, no, no, not at all," she said.

Alex stopped chewing and looked at my mother. "Oh, Mrs. Shimoda. You should have told me you didn't like the diner's food."

I sighed. "That's not the point, Alex."

"No?" Alex raised his eyebrows.

"I think we'd like, at some point, to eat something cooked at home."

"Of course. Everyone likes home cooking."

"If we ever have a kitchen, that is."

"Just eat," my mother told me, her chopsticks busy inside a container of sweet-and-sour pork.

"Oh, I get it." Alex plopped a pancake onto his plate, smoothing out the edges. "I get it. You're trying to tell me the renovation is taking a long time."

"Well, isn't it?"

Alex's face twitched.

"I agree, it's taking a bit longer than I had originally

planned," he said. "But I haven't encountered any problems that should concern you, I can tell you that."

"Where are all the cupboard doors?" I asked.

"My supplier pal's a bit slow. He promises me the doors will come in by next Wednesday."

I squirted a blob of duck sauce onto my plate. "Is your supplier pal responsible for getting us the oven that doesn't heat up?"

My mother made a choking sound, nearly spitting a small mouthful of food onto her plate. "This is terrible," she exclaimed breathlessly.

"Oh, Mrs. Shimoda, please. It isn't that bad," Alex said, his voice low and concerned.

"No, no, look at this." My mother picked up a newspaper from the floor, folded it, and showed us a page. PAVAROTTI FALLS SHY OF HIGH NOTE the headline read.

"He missed the high C's when singing the part of Tonio in Donizetti's *Daughter of the Regiment*," my mother said, scanning the article. "'Mr. Pavarotti had not sung the Donizetti role in twenty-two years,'" she read, "'and since then age and a heavier repertory have robbed his voice of some of its agility. It seems he has given up his crown as King of the High C's.'"

Alex looked at me and shrugged. My mother seemed lost in the words, reading on, breathing deeply.

"Oh, poor Luciano!" she murmured, lowering the newspaper to the table. "It must be so difficult for him, getting older. So much pressure, and he's such a proud man. But he has to remember one thing. He must remember."

"What's that?" Alex asked, wiping the corners of his mouth with a paper napkin.

My mother looked at both of us. "He is not a *tenore di forza!*" she nearly shouted.

"He must remember that," she continued in a lower voice, patting the newspaper against her palm and knocking her chopsticks to the floor. "He's a lyric tenor, with a sweet, tender voice, always using his diaphragm lightly. Forget about those dramatic tenor roles! Forget Verdi's *Don Carlos!* Forget striving for *Otello!*"

She bent over, retrieved her chopsticks with a tiny grunt and waved them in the air in triumph. "That's what I will tell him," she said, straightening up in her chair. "I'll tell him, 'Luciano, you're not a *tenore di forza!*' "

And with that, she dug into her sweet-and-sour pork with renewed vigor.

I wished then that I could be like my mother and find happiness in so many small things. Her passion seemed to give her heightened sensibilities while I felt I could never summon more than superficial pleasure—the brief, trancelike comfort of eating ice cream, the fleeting, artificial sadness of a sentimental movie. All I could really remember about my dreams of being an architect were my reasons for dismantling them: a fear of failing, a fear of not making enough money, a fear of discovering that I couldn't love anything enough to make it the center of my life.

As my mother and Alex ate their Chinese food, I felt faded, out of focus, like a photograph left too long in the sun.

ONE NIGHT, AFTER a long dinner shift, I returned home so late all the lights were out on our street except for a dim lamp in our living room window. I trudged up the stairs from the garage, the smell of grease from the steak-house following me like a stray cat. I went to the kitchen, eager for something cool and clear to drink, but when I opened the refrigerator, I spotted the beer. It was wedged between a carton of juice and a jar of mayonnaise, and I reached out to touch the cold glass.

Whenever my father mowed the lawn, he'd mow the entire yard at once, curving his way around the many trees and trotting down the straightaways as if led by an eager dog. He never stopped, unless the engine died, and then he'd pull the starter cord, yanking it furiously behind him while a great blue vein pushed its way up under the skin of his neck. Even when our neighbors graduated to tractor-like mowers, Pappa stuck by his greasy machine. During the summer he'd mow the lawn every Sunday before lunch, dressed in a sleeveless undershirt and a pair of gray pants from an old suit.

His reward waited in the refrigerator, a cooling brown bottle of beer. I was never sure who put it there to chill, he or my mother. Seeing a beer there now, years later, I had a sudden feeling that my father had returned home. That, of course, was impossible.

The next morning I showered vigorously, washing my hair twice, massaging the shampoo into a billowing lather, scrubbing my skin pink with a rough loofah sponge. When I went downstairs, my mother was sitting at the kitchen table with decorating magazines spread out in front of her as if the answers to all life's questions could be found in one or another issue of *Architectural Digest*.

"You must have come back late last night," she said. "I was up until midnight, looking at these bathrooms."

I brightened. I'd always wanted a Japanese-style bath in our house, with a deep, square tub where you could sit up to your chin in hot water.

"Do you think we might be able to install an ofuro? I've always wanted one."

My mother looked up and laughed. "Heavens, no! I'd much prefer a wonderful Italian marble tub. Much more impressive."

I shrugged, pulling a comb through my wet hair, and sat down, my stiff terry-cloth bathrobe bunched around my waist.

My mother watched me, turning a page. "Did I get you that?" she asked.

"A few Christmases ago," I replied, checking for a crisp apple among the soft ones in the fruit bowl. Finding none, I poured myself a glass of juice and drank.

"That's a good bathrobe. It was expensive."

My mother folded a page corner and showed me a photo of a modern bathroom with a sunken green marble tub. "Beautiful, don't you think? I never considered green."

"When did you start drinking beer?" I asked, combing my hair back with quick, wet slaps.

"Beer? You know I don't drink beer," she said and looked up from her magazine for a moment, her lips slightly parting. "Oh, the beer," she murmured, looking back down. "Alex is working today. I thought it might be nice for him. He works hard."

"The last thing Alex needs is to drink beer. He's not so fantastic even when he's sober."

"It's just a gesture."

I got up, slid my empty glass into a bucket full of dirty dishes in the sink and filled a pot with water. As I set it on the stove I paused.

"Something's different," I said, turning on the flame under the pot.

"It's a new kind of range. Special for entertaining."

"How so?"

"It's got a salamander broiler. High-heat glass jets. More space between burners." My mother spoke methodically, as if reading from a list.

"A what broiler?"

"A salamander broiler. Very strong heat. So when I make my zabaglione, I can just stick it under there to brown before serving. So easy. I told Alex about my singing group gatherings, and he suggested it might make things easier."

"For your singing group parties? But you've never had more than five people over at a time."

My mother returned to her magazines, turning the pages at a leisurely pace. "He also installed a garbage compactor," she continued, "and an ice maker that makes twenty-five pounds of ice a day."

"You're planning to build an igloo?" I asked.

"When the renovation is completed, I will want to throw a few big parties, in celebration of the new house. It'll be worth it. I'm also thinking about adding a new bathroom."

"We don't need a new bathroom."

"Of course we could use a new bathroom. We've been talking about that for years." My mother nodded blankly. "A big green bathroom," she said, her finger tracing a photo of a cavernous bathtub.

PAPPA NEVER TOLD me anything at all. He was an attractive man, slim with a large, intelligent forehead, so I assumed he never had problems with girls. He liked Western food. He once grabbed a pencil from me and drew my profile with just one dark stroke. ("That's me, that's exactly me!" I cried. He never drew anything for me again.) Occasionally he threw something from his past out to me, which I would grab and squeeze for all its possibilities.

While watching television when I was seven, Pappa said, "We once took in a stray." His lips left his cigar just long enough to say that. Then he got up and went to smoke in his den. I watched the rest of the program looking for dogs.

A few years later, he told me in passing that he had had another brother. He mentioned it casually, as if remarking on the shape of a cloud. "It was an unusual situation," he said while we were raking leaves in the backyard. "He was sent away. My mother couldn't afford to keep three sons. She had to pick two of us."

He worked like a machine, systematically creating little leaf piles at various critical locations, then melding them together.

His words were weightless as the leaves, and he kept working. Nothing in his face suggested to me that the memory was difficult; his eyes remained fixed on the end of his rake.

"How?" I asked, not knowing what else to say.

Pappa began combining two piles. "She just did," he said. "Those were difficult times." Then he coughed with a burst of frosty air.

We raked in silence after that.

Months later, a call came early in the morning. Charlotte and I were eating breakfast, poking at bowls of cold cereal, while my mother ran upstairs to get my father, who was sleeping. They made a lot of noise, my mother telling Pappa to hurry and my father trying to wrap a robe around himself and secure his feet in slippers as he came shuffling down the stairs. I remember his face from that morning, his eyes swollen from sleep, his wavy hair matted against one side of his face.

"Hurry, hurry," my mother said again.

Charlotte and I continued to eat. We didn't make much of Pappa's phone call. Relatives in Japan would occasionally ring us early in the morning, to tell us someone had had a stroke, or a baby had been born, or an earthquake had just missed them. After speaking for a minute or so, Pappa hung up, his hand lingering on the receiver.

"Your grandmother is coming to live with us," he said to the wall.

He spoke matter-of-factly, his voice raspy, unexcited. He looked at us. My mother and sister were motionless.

She had come to stay with us before, for a few weeks at a time, a foreign presence who put a blue toothbrush and a tiny tube of Japanese toothpaste beside our bathroom sink, set her ornate silver comb and mirror on a table next to her bed, and ground her cigarette stubs at the bottom of ashtrays we'd find everywhere. She didn't speak any English, so her communication was limited to crooked smiles indicating "Do you like this?" when giving us presents, and frowning for "Should you be doing that?" when our parents were away. Charlotte and I would sit and observe her as she watched television or read a magazine, taking in her shiny, black patent-leather shoes, the mound of hair pinned in a messy bun on top of her head, the humplike shape of her upper spine. My mother hated her (for her aloofness, her closeness to Pappa, her disdain), and her dislike was strong enough to become my own.

That evening, after Pappa returned home from work, he went to the kitchen and talked to my mother about renovating the house and adding a new bathroom. Neither Charlotte nor I were fluent enough to participate, and my father's conversation, as usual, became part of the background noise as we sat in the living room, watching television.

After we finished dinner, my father opened another bottle of red wine and poured himself a glassful. Pierre had retreated to his bedroom, and I heard his radio and the *thuk, thuk, thuk* of a basketball thrown against the wall.

"What if we built a bathroom upstairs for you two?" Pappa asked, his fingers toying with the stem of his wineglass. "Would that make you happy?"

His eyes were watery and unfocused as he waited for our response. We squirmed, uncertain of what to say, while my mother remained silent, listening as she washed dishes in the sink, the china and glass clinking softly under soapy water. Pappa finished his wine and began to describe his mother's house.

It was a simple, wooden two-story box, squeezed in between two large buildings on a busy street in Kyoto, with loose slats on the outside and holes in the paper shoji screens inside. Termites had begun eating away at the walls, while weeds and grass flourished atop the tiled roof. The toilet was a deep hole in the ground. A precarious stairway led to the attic, where my grandmother kept Christmas tinsel hanging year-round. The attic steps were now too steep for her to climb, he said. Robbers had recently broken in the back door and taken my grandmother's television and ten cartons of her cigarettes, he continued.

"We were very lucky she was out when that happened," Pappa said.

My mother squeezed a sponge dry and wiped the rim of the sink, her lips pressed tightly together. Occasionally, she glanced at my father as he spoke, as if ready to interject.

"It won't be a problem," Pappa continued. He leaned back in his chair and took a puff of his cigar.

"Maybe not for you," my mother replied. She was standing facing us now, the sink sparklingly clean, her arms folded across her chest.

My father looked up, irritation dancing over his normally calm features.

"She's my mother," he said, his cigar now hanging from his fingers, unlit.

He pushed open a box of matches and picked out a matchstick. The *thuk, thuk, thuk* from Pierre's room continued, and my father's smoke was soon feeling its way around the room. Pappa's mother never came to live with us, and we never heard Pappa speak of it again.

THE YARD WE used to rake every fall was now covered with the brown leaves of several seasons. Alex and my mother were standing on top of the hill, as they often did when discussing the house.

Alex turned and smiled as I headed in their direction. "It's the beautiful daughter," he said, and my mother laughed.

"No, my older one, Charlotte, is beautiful. This daughter is the charming one."

Alex was wearing a faded purple workshirt and black jeans. He chewed gum like a duty.

"Very charming," he said.

SOMETIMES, FOR A brief moment, I felt happy living at home. These moments would come in the morning, when I'd wake in my brother's bedroom to the smell of breakfast cooking downstairs, the early sun filtering through a tree near the window, filling the room with soft, airy light. My mother would be in the middle of an operatic aria, the clanging of pans occasionally subsiding while she worked through a particularly difficult series of notes.

But that feeling would quickly pass. Our family had long ago dissolved. All the rituals my mother performed—setting the table, getting the newspaper—were just for us two. I began to wonder what would happen to her if this remaining bit of family were to disappear.

I feared people could smell the vulnerability in our home: the man checking the gas meter, the UPS driver whistling up the front steps, the salesmen pestering on the phone. I felt unprotected from the sharp edges of the world. Late at night, I imagined that I could hear the tumult of families around me, the muffled sound of couples arguing, children crying, dogs howling, a subway's distant rumbling. I wondered what it would be like were my father still there, if he could shield me from my fears, or if he would be as apprehensive as myself.

MY MOTHER WAS the only person I knew who bathed in the middle of the day. Her need to bathe would come suddenly, not necessarily corresponding with sweat or dirt, and she'd prepare for it as if performing an ancient ritual. Window and door were closed to keep the steam from escaping. The water had to be scalding to the touch. A clean hand towel, white, folded in thirds, was placed as a headrest on the bathtub rim. After reclining in the tub, my mother would let a trickle from the faucet dribble down to keep the water hot. From downstairs, I pictured the tiny rivulet, its purposeful burble echoing hazily against the tile.

My mother began singing scales in the bath. She always practiced scales while bathing, never singing songs. I imagined her in the tub, blithely spreading the washcloth over her chest, her knees occasionally breaking the water's surface.

Meanwhile, Alex and I were in the kitchen deciding the fate of the Formica table and leatherette chairs.

"Throw all of this away," Alex said.

"Just because it's old doesn't necessarily mean we should throw it away," I replied. By destroying the vestiges of our former life, we were letting something else in the house quickly evaporate.

"There's good old, and there's bad old, and this is very bad old," he said.

But I suddenly missed the dried spaghetti sauce that seemed forever to encrust the old stovetop; I even missed the matching splatters against the wall that looked as if my mother had flung her wooden spoon about like a conductor's baton. Gone were the unplumbed depths of a twenty-year-old Frigidaire that offered up wet, rotting vegetables and furry slices of bread. The cabinet drawers had been emptied of pens from vacation motels and keys to forgotten cars and doors. The new cupboards bore clear, unblemished complexions, and lined our kitchen like blank faces. The refrigerator's freezer heaved fresh ice at specific intervals. Alex had replaced the worn linoleum floor with even brown tiles, and the dishwasher was now obedient and ploddingly predictable. While open surfaces and shiny modern appliances were easily pleasing, like the clean decor of a new hotel, the soul of the kitchen was gone.

Alex picked up one of the chairs and turned it over. My parents had purchased the set after my father made his first big sale of subway cars to New York's Metropolitan Transit Authority. They had decided to buy something colorful and big, something that would have been impossible to own in Japan. I liked the kitchen set, particularly the chairs, each shaped like an egg, with a quarter cut out to make a seat. The table was a huge white oval mounted on a scuffed mushroom stem.

"The swivel of this chair is all worn away," Alex continued. I could hear my mother as she launched into arpeggios. After pausing a moment, she switched to a minor key. She sounded good, her pitch accurate, though the magnifying acoustics of the bathroom made her high notes sound like shrieks.

"I can take these to the dump this afternoon," Alex added. "I have a friend in the kitchen-supply business. He can get you another set, with modern, plastic chairs, great quality, at a good price."

Before, there had been so much of our decaying house I hated, but it was difficult for me now to be specific about what it was that had been so bad. Certainly, there were parts of the house that desperately needed to be cleaned or fixed. But replacing the objects that had accrued through the years was too blatant an attempt at erasing the past. No matter the pain of what had gone before, memories filled things with meaning.

LIGHT POURED INTO my mother's kitchen. The new floor-to-ceiling windows captured every bit of light outside, from the gray white of the overcast sky to an overturned wheelbarrow's metal bottom in the backyard. Alex had painted the window frames white. I sat by them, suspicious, having argued earlier that such a big expanse of glass would make the kitchen drafty. But the windows were solid, like walls.

"I'm making this perfect," my mother said, scraping away bits of dried paint from the window with a razor blade.

"I think Alex should be doing that," I told her.

"Have you seen the new sink? It's truly something. Here, watch."

She abandoned the paint-flecked window and walked briskly to the sink—cream-colored and huge, as big as a baby bathtub. A sturdy nozzle was hooked up to one side, and at the press of a button, the steady stream of water turned into a spray. My mother switched the nozzle from steady stream to spray a few times.

Everything in the kitchen had changed. The walls were a pale green, a pinkish sheen rose from the pickled-wood cabinets, and the floor tiles, like saddle leather, were hard and soft at the same time. The stainless steel stove shone like a platinum altar.

My mother darted about the kitchen on her small feet, moving from the stove to the window, not sure which needed cleaning more. I heard Alex's truck pulling into the driveway, its tires spitting loose gravel. My mother smoothed her hair with her hands. "Oh, I have to talk to Alex," she said.

She untied the strings of her stained apron as she rushed out of the kitchen. Soon, I could hear her voice, becoming high and girlish, and a moment later she was laughing at one of his silly jokes.

THREE

Pappa had always been interested in our development, but even as a child I suspected his attention was rooted more in scientific curiosity than anything particularly paternal. When we got colds, he'd prod our mouths with tongue depressors, examining our throats and tonsils. He plotted our changing shoe size on graph paper and once even weighed us before and after urinating. We participated obediently in this research, although never quite certain what the results were used for, or what they might mean. "You're the children of a very intelligent man," my mother would tell us by means of explanation, but the dismissive tone of her voice meant that she didn't really understand what Pappa was doing either.

One of my father's pet projects was the height wall. He had picked a spot in the dining room where we were measured next to a glass cabinet filled with rows of tiny Japanese dolls. We stood against the wall, and my father would put an empty cigar box on our heads, holding it in place after we moved so he could draw a line. Each horizontal stroke was followed by dates and names written in precise, capital letters, clear enough for us to read. The dates Pappa picked to measure us seemed arbitrary, but eventually a pattern emerged. CHARLOTTE 5/30/67 hovered near the bottom (my sister's height when she was two years old), just above the one for our dog Giuseppe (put to sleep 1/13/88). The intense concentration of lines at the bottom loosened near the middle and suddenly jumped when we hit our teens.

Like a tourist, my mother stood in front of the wall peering through a camera my father had left behind. While her left hand was still turning the lens to focus, the shutter snapped.

"Heavens," she said, surprised. "Go ahead, Alex," she added, cocking back the film.

The three of us stood motionless in the empty living room, and then Alex slowly began to stir his brush in the open can of thick white paint.

"Maybe you should take another one," he advised, "just to be sure."

My mother snapped again at the wall and stepped back. Alex started at the top, painting over the highest line, PIERRE 9/23/89, the date my brother surpassed my father and the year we stopped measuring. He approached the part that was mine, the tallest female in the family. Below that, the wall was smudged from all of us sidling up against it, the cigar box balanced on our heads. Even my mother's height was recorded. She would come in from the kitchen to watch us, an apron wound tightly around her waist, and my father would grab her awkwardly, both of them laughing.

After a few quick strokes, the lines chronicling nearly twenty-five years of growth vanished, and the wall was once again blank.

"Well, that's that," my mother said. She remained cheery although Alex had been quiet while performing his task. She walked back to the kitchen wearing the camera on a strap around her wrist.

Alex touched up the paint where pencil marks peeped through the first coat. "Short family," he said. Suddenly, the family ritual seemed faintly ridiculous to me. Our private battle to the top, wide open until Pierre had his growth spurt, would have been easily won by Alex or just about any outsider who walked in the door.

"Where's she?" Alex was pointing to a stubborn spot where my sister seemed to have peaked, hitting the same spot year after year as the black pencil mark thickened.

"She's a banker in Chicago."

"Ah. The Windy City."

I began wrapping three wooden wise men with newspaper. My mother had put them out on the mantelpiece one Christmas many years ago and liked them so much she decided to leave them out all year round. I started with the one bearing gifts that looked like tiny golf balls.

"Married?" Alex asked.

"Nope."

"Maybe I should marry her," he said.

I threw him a nasty look, not sure whether or not he was joking, but he remained engrossed in thought. "She's very picky," I told him.

"And you?" Alex asked.

I looked at him. "What about me?"

"Boyfriend?" Alex smiled while he continued to paint peacefully, his eyes focused on the wall.

"Actually, I'm married."

Alex stopped painting for a moment. "Really? Where's your husband?"

"You know how men are. In love with you one minute, dump you the next."

Alex's smile disappeared. "You're kidding."

"And for another woman, too. I was crushed," I said flatly.

"That's terrible. But you mustn't let one bad apple make you sour on men in general. No sir. There are plenty of good ones out there."

"I'm just kidding around, Alex," I said.

"Oh." Alex raised his eyebrows and closed his lips tightly. "Well, I guess that's a good thing."

I flushed. "I just don't like talking about my personal life."

"It's not like I'm about to ask you out on a date or anything," Alex said and wiggled his bushy eyebrows until they looked like bouncing white hamsters.

"What about your brother?" he continued. "Is he around?"

"He lives in Milan."

"I see." The contractor pursed his lips just as he did when deciding how much to charge for lugging our garbage to the dump. "Excuse me for saying this, but Pierre's a pretty weird name for a Japanese kid."

I sighed. "He was born during my mother's French period. My sister and I were born before that, during her English period. We were named after the Brontës."

Alex looked blankly at me.

"Have you ever heard of the Brontës?" I asked.

"Where's that?"

"Never mind," I replied.

Alex cleared his throat and continued with his questions. "So, why's Pierre in Milan? Shouldn't he be in Paris or something?"

"Although Pierre was born during my mother's French period, he was more influenced by her most recent Italian period. He's studying art there."

"Oh," Alex said, after a while.

My mother began to sing in the kitchen. Her voice shimmered into the living room like a choirboy's, soft but surprisingly clear.

"So, what do you do?" Alex asked me, cocking his head to one side as he repainted a spot on the wall.

"I'm a waitress," I said in a high-pitched voice that wasn't my own. "I'm still looking for other work though."

Charlotte and I both took tests in high school to see what career paths each of us should follow. My sister's results suggested she should become an advertising executive. Mine said I should become a florist. I could understand how a test might point someone toward advertising, but I couldn't see how a test could conclude that someone should work with cut flowers.

"Waitressing's a good job. Nothing to be ashamed of," Alex said. "What kind of place?"

"A Japanese steakhouse. They cook on a grill in front of the customers—like Benihana."

Alex brightened and flung his arms around, as if playing the drums, flicking drops of paint onto the floor. "I've seen them, with those knives. Do they have to go to school for that?"

I looked at a large drop of white paint, the size of a dime, which had landed on a corner of the carpet uncovered by a tarp. As if bidden by my stare, Alex bent over and dabbed at the paint with a rag.

"Some chefs spend a few weeks at a restaurant camp in Florida, but they mostly make it up as they go along," I replied. "Did you go to school for painting?"

He ignored my question and rose to his toes to reach a high spot on the wall. From the kitchen, my mother was attempting to sing the mad aria from *Lucia di Lammermoor.* "I think you and your mother both need a man in the house," he said, straining. "Things feel out of control here. It doesn't seem right with only you two around."

Ironically, there had rarely been a man around, even when my parents were married. Pappa frequently traveled alone out of the country and slept late when he was home. My mother tried to fill in by doing more than a mother needed to, making crepes on weekday mornings and ironing my underwear. Yet, unfettered by another's input, her parenting became increasingly free-form. I felt empowered when I went out with my high school friends, knowing I could drink whatever I chose, or stay out all night if I wanted. The only men consistently present in our lives were disembodied: Luciano Pavarotti, Plácido Domingo, Carlo Bergonzi, Leo Nucci. Their voices followed me around the house, singing of love and betrayal.

"Smells like dog," Alex said, freezing at attention and sniffing the air. "Right here." He was standing in front of the air conditioner.

"Our dog liked to sleep there when it got hot," I said, taping the box shut and running my fingers over the top, embarrassed by the smell of old urine and dog hair. "He died a few years ago."

"It's like he never left," Alex said, laughing.

"My mother likes to have him around. It comforts her."

"She likes this smell?"

I shook my head and pointed to a wooden box, wrapped in a mauve silk cloth, on the mantelpiece. Alex looked at me blankly.

"Giuseppe's ashes," I said. "My mother can't decide where to bury him."

"He's in there?"

"Since 1988," I replied.

Alex whistled. "That's a long time to have a dead dog in your living room," he said, slowly putting his brush down. He stepped away from the air conditioner and began examining the room.

"I'm thinking satin finish for the trim," he said loudly, so my mother could hear from the kitchen. "Trade eggshell. It's pretty expensive and needs careful brushwork, but it's the best. And if I paint the ceiling a slightly whiter white than the walls, the room will look bigger."

"Yes, yes, that's a good idea," my mother called out. "I want the room to feel big and airy. I want it to become a different place."

For as long as I could remember, the room had been a shrine to Danish Modern, with a white floor lamp on a curved stem like a limp tulip, and a modular couch that

worked its way around the room like a swollen uphol-
stered worm. In the corner a huge, opaque white plastic
orb, three feet in diameter, lit up like a giant glowing
Ping-Pong ball. The carpet was a blinding ocean of electric blue.

THE SMELL OF olive oil and garlic wafted in from
the kitchen as my mother tossed pasta with fresh basil and
a little anchovy. She hadn't really cooked since the renovation, hoping to preserve the artificially clean state of the
room. No grouper osso bucco, which involved deboning
the fish and grinding fresh Italian herbs with mortar and
pestle; no braised-rabbit risotto, which involved so much
dredging and reducing that afterward the kitchen looked
like a battlefield.

After sprinkling chopped basil on top of each plate, she
called me in to eat.

"Alex, are you hungry, too? Would you like some
pasta?" she asked.

"No thanks. Smells wonderful, but I never eat when I'm
in the middle of something," he called back.

My mother smiled. "Such a proper reply," she murmured.

"I feel like we should be in *Architectural Digest*," I said.
The kitchen table was a spotless white oval on which the
noodles sat steaming on bright blue plates.

My mother sat down and blew on her capellini. "This is

quite nice, I must admit. Much nicer than when your father was around."

I nodded, chewing a mouthful of hot noodles silently. She had lived among the remnants of her life with Pappa for years, and I now wondered if their sudden absence made her feel more alone.

"In many ways, your father has always been an undisciplined man," my mother continued.

"I know—he's lazy," I said, poking at my pasta with my fork. "You always tell me that."

"No, not lazy. Undisciplined." My mother paused, watching through the window as a charcoal gray squirrel shot across the yard and zipped up a tree.

"I don't think there's a difference," I told her.

"Just before I married your father, he was living with another woman," she added.

"You mean his mother," I said, suddenly alert.

"Yes. And then with a young woman. He's had many women, you know."

I rested my fork across my half-eaten plate of food and looked out the window. Rain was beginning to fall.

"That's a stupid story," I said.

My mother laughed. "Well, I didn't make it up. You have to understand what kind of man your father is." She continued to eat, sucking the long noodles into her mouth without a sound.

• • •

THOUGH DIVORCED FOR two and a half years, my father still hadn't settled into a new home. Instead, he lived in a succession of hotels—each night pulling open crisp bedsheets, bleach and starch disguising the fact that countless strangers had slept in them before. He drank from the minibar, left glasses scattered around the room, and dropped damp towels on the bathroom floor. All he needed to do was take a long walk and the room would be completely cleared of his presence, reset like bowling pins. Pappa apparently loved that life.

When I was growing up, he had written me letters on stationery from hotels around the world. The Peninsula in Hong Kong, The Château Frontenac in Quebec, The Crillon in Paris. He never said what he was doing in those places, and once I laid out the letters in the order they had come, looking for the logic of his travels. Why did he go from Melbourne to Brasília? The letters asked uninspired questions and provided strange bits of information. "How are you? Are you well? There is a fruit here called the rambutan that looks like a hairy Ping-Pong ball. I find there are many old people walking the streets. Love, Father."

I often thought about living with Pappa. We could live in hotel suites, liberated, each in our own room. The meals would always be perfect and exactly what we wanted that day, rolled in to our rooms on tables adorned with tiny vases of flowers. Life would be distilled to simple acts carried out amidst furniture picked out by a stranger.

WHEN I RETURNED home from work that night, there was a postcard on the kitchen table. My mother was at the sink, her back toward me, washing dishes. It wasn't until I sat down at the table that I realized the card was from my father.

"I can't believe that you are still in contact with him," my mother said, her words barely audible above the water streaming into the sink.

I had already intercepted two letters from my father, but had started working lunch shifts and could no longer meet the eleven o'clock mail. I watched my mother dry her hands and walk out of the room. A moment later the door to her bedroom clicked shut behind her. I knew she would sink into a dark, trembling mood that would confine her for a day like a tunnel.

The postcard was from the Imperial Hotel in Tokyo. "Hello from Japan. The bread here is surprisingly delicious. The wind smells of the sea. I will soon settle down. Love, Father."

That sounded promising. A year earlier, he had sent photographs of a Louis XIII–style château for sale in Brittany. "Groomed gardens, vaulted ceilings, a ballroom," he wrote on the back of one. "This is beyond beauty."

The owner, a countess, ran a bed-and-breakfast to make ends meet but now was tired and old and wanted to sell. "From chandeliers to oven mitts," my father had written, "it's all there." I was sure this would be his home.

As ALEX PAINTED the ceiling in the living room, my mother perused her battered opera records. She pored over librettos and listened to her records over and over until she had memorized the Italian lyrics phonetically. She'd sing the arias and love duets from *Daughter of the Regiment, Tosca, Rigoletto,* and *L'elisir d'amore* while cooking and cleaning, and those songs were the first thing I'd hear in the morning. Even I could hum the melodies.

She kept these records meticulously organized beneath the record player. The mahogany stereo console sat alone against one wall of the living room, like the black lacquered altar that dominated the sitting room in the house where she grew up. She treated the actual records terribly when listening to them, handling them like plates, stacking one atop another, and carelessly plunking down the needle. But when she wanted to find a particular performer or composer, she knew its exact location. Domingo, after Debussy, before Donizetti. She'd sit in the middle of the living room, listening to a record with eyes closed, as serene as a Buddha.

Secretly, I longed to feel a similar passion. While she plunged headfirst into things, I kept life at arm's length, never delving too deeply into anything—an observer of my own life.

Lately, my mother played records not only for entertainment, but to educate Alex as he worked around her. She slammed a record down onto the turntable, and after missing the beginning with the needle, successfully hit the scratchy start on her second try.

"Plácido, Plácido," she said, gazing at the record cover as the music warbled from the speakers. She flipped the cover over to see the song list. "Such an overachiever," she said, showing me Domingo's face. "Can't you tell by the boastful way that he looks?"

I nodded, taking the cover from her and wiping its edges with a rag.

"After singing his first *Otello* in the late 1970s, he completely recast himself as a heldentenor," my mother continued.

"Heldentenor?" Alex repeated, standing on a ladder, paintbrush in hand. "What does that mean?"

My mother looked up at him and paused. For a moment I worried that she couldn't answer and the reputation she had fostered would fall from her like a heavy drape.

I handed back the album cover and pointed to a corner of the ceiling. "You missed a spot there, Alex," I said.

"Heldentenor," my mother said, using a fingernail to scrape off a price tag from a corner of the cover. "A tenor with a strong, dramatic voice. Well suited for heavy Wagnerian roles such as Parsifal or Tristan. In other words, a heroic tenor."

Alex looked at her and nodded. "Very interesting," he said, turning to dab at the ceiling corner with a brush. Pleased, my mother began perusing the E's.

WE WERE NEVER meant to be Americans. My parents' move to the U.S. was only going to be for a few years, five at the most. Even when I was a child, my mother treated her American life as an educational experience, a sort of sociological experiment. "Fill up please, fill up please," she'd chant while driving to town, swerving uneasily around squirrels on Quaker Road. She'd carefully enunciate the *l*'s right up until she rolled down her window at the gas station and the pimply face of a teenage boy peered in.

"What'll it be?" he would ask.

When my father returned from work, she'd tell him how her *l*'s had become *r*'s, how the word "fill" turned to "fear." "There is so much to learn before we leave," she'd say. I wasn't sure if Pappa really listened to her stories. He'd drink a glass of wine and eat a handful of macadamia nuts, his head tilted at an angle as if trying to listen with one good ear, but would say nothing in return.

Each Saturday morning, Charlotte and I attended Japanese language school in Riverdale, as religiously as if it were church. We made fun of the other Japanese students at school, the boys in tight shorts and white ankle socks, the girls tittering like birds, but we did so a little jealously, alone. While we struggled with the ideograms for tree and rock, our American friends sailed around on bicycles, faces upturned to the sky.

One Saturday morning, Charlotte and I dressed and

went downstairs for breakfast, character workbooks and flashcards in hand. My mother was in the kitchen drinking coffee, wrapped in her bathrobe.

"You can go back to sleep," she told us.

"School is canceled?" Charlotte asked hopefully.

My mother shook her head, folding a paper towel and slipping it between her coffee cup and saucer. "No more school," she said.

"It burned down?" I asked.

"No. Just no more school," my mother replied.

She looked at us with a solemn face, as if not yet convinced herself. I remember wondering why she looked so sad. In time, we forgot what Saturdays had been like when we couldn't go out and play like the other children on our street. It wasn't until much later that I realized what my mother had done that day, snipping the final tie that connected us with her home.

"WELL, THAT'S IT, *finito*," Alex said, stepping away from the ladder and surveying the living room with his hands on his hips. "Looks pretty good, pretty darn good."

The new white paint gave off a matte glow. The windows, stripped of curtains, let in a large rectangle of sky. My mother emerged from the kitchen, drying her hands on a dishtowel, and nodded her approval. "Simply lovely," she said. "The feeling of the house has changed. Completely."

I bent down and pulled away a portion of the tarp in front of me. The edge of the tarp was faintly outlined on the carpet in specks of white.

My mother stood near Alex, who was closing the lid on a can of paint. Suddenly, he turned to her.

"Have you ever considered weather stripping?" he asked.

I flipped the tarp back further to reveal speckles of white in the shape of a trapezoid that had been left uncovered. Beyond that, a distinct white bootprint.

"I'm not even certain what weather stripping is," my mother replied, though her voice had turned wooden.

"In the winter, your door shrinks, creating a gap which lets in cold air," Alex explained, crossing his arms across his chest and rubbing his shoulders vigorously with his hands. "If you install metal spring strips around the doors, the air can't get in. It's a real money saver. The strips also stop doors from swelling in the summer, so they don't get stuck."

"That sounds wonderful," my mother said flatly.

I picked up most of the tarp.

Alex whipped out a rag, bent over, and began scrubbing at the dried paint. "Oh, this'll come up, no problem," he said.

"Alex, don't worry," my mother told him. "The furniture will cover that."

I looked at her. "No it won't. The couch doesn't go anywhere near there."

A stony silence followed as Alex rubbed the carpet furiously.

"Anyway," my mother continued, "I've been thinking about removing the carpet."

"You have?"

"Yes, I have been thinking about a hardwood floor in this room," she said and looked at me defiantly. "The wall-to-wall carpeting was your father's idea, anyway. He thought it was so American."

We all stood silent and still for a moment.

"Coast sitka spruce?" asked Alex, stuffing the rag into his back pocket. "Ponderosa pine? Eastern hemlock-tamarack? It's up to you, Mrs. Shimoda."

"Ponderosa pine. I love the way that sounds. Quite musical, isn't it?"

I dropped the tarp and left the room rather than expressing my disgust.

When I came back ten minutes later, Alex was jumping up and down, his dusty workboots thumping on the carpeted floor like a heartbeat. "Are the windows shaking?" he asked, jumping more lightly.

My mother stared at the living room's large glass pane and nodded vaguely. "Seems to be so," she replied.

He suddenly stopped, as if waiting for an echo, and we were all quiet.

"Is this a bad thing?" my mother asked.

Alex scratched his head. "Well, it's something I've been

concerned about. The floor joists are undersized, or maybe even cracked. And the floor seems a bit bouncy. If we're going to do the floor, maybe we should replace or reinforce the joists first. Anyway, I've got some wood samples in the back of the truck. Care to take a look?"

My mother flushed pink and nodded. "Love to," she said.

They went out the front door and crossed our lawn, Alex walking backward while speaking, gesturing as if in pantomime, my mother listening with her hands in her pockets as they headed for the truck, parked in the driveway. I watched Alex reach into the back and pull out what looked like a large key chain with wood samples. He flicked to one and said something, flicked ahead to another, pointed, and laughed. A gust of wind blew through the pink and white trees across the street, sending a few petals floating through the air.

W H A T   I   H A D liked best about Ben was his fearlessness. His exuberance was swashbuckling in scope. He wasn't terribly athletic, but he loved tennis, thrashing about the court like he was cutting down sugarcane. He wrote strange, avant-garde plays for an experimental theater company, never flinching when only a few friends would show up for an uncomfortable performance. His Mandarin was elementary and awkward, but he insisted on trying it out whenever we ate at a Chinese restaurant, much to the amusement of the waiters. "They only speak Cantonese," he'd explain to me apologetically.

Meeting him was like being hit in the face with a snowball; my senses had been jarred awake, tingling with irritation as if a deadened outer layer had been suddenly peeled away. College was no longer simply classes, laundry, and regular calls home. Ben took me to a gay disco and a taxidermy museum a few towns away; he insisted on trying the food at every eating hall on campus and dragged me regularly to the top of the school bell tower for a bird's-eye view of campus. Within a week, he was sleeping in my bed and had reduced my laundry regime to cold-water washes of mixed loads.

I watched rain pelt the window of the bus as it hummed quietly on its way downtown. Ben's head tapped my shoulder at irregular intervals, until he finally gave in to the pull of sleep and dropped his head against me. In the short time I had known Ben, I had discovered a few key things about him: He was violently allergic to nuts, he loved the singer Tom Jones, and he could sleep in anything that moved. The one time we went skiing together he nodded off riding the gondola, the back of his head softly banging against the glass.

As we neared our stop, I jiggled my shoulder to rouse him. For a brief moment, I wondered if this was what marriage could possibly be about, not so much a romantic union, but a process in which you discover more and more

about your spouse, chipping away at expectations and ap-
pearances, until finally an individual you never imagined
is completely unearthed.

"Wake up," I said.

Ben's head jerked away from me, as if his cheek had
grazed a hot frying pan.

"Wha?" he gasped, straining open his eyes as widely as
possible.

"We're the next stop."

"Next stop, next stop," he mumbled, lids lowering.

"The movie theater," I reminded him.

"Yeah. Yeah."

I thought about my mother and father, married for what
now seemed like a brief twenty-eight years. Discarded expectations had mounted into a pile so high that it eventually separated them. I wanted some kind of reassurance
from Ben, a sign that exposing ourselves was a process of
clarification, not something that would get in our way. It
was silly of me at this point in our relationship to think
that we would end up together, but I suddenly felt afraid
that the more we got to know each other, the less either of
us would find to love.

Ben's eyes flickered open, as if he heard my thoughts,
but then closed again. He fell back asleep, his body bobbing and swaying to the rhythms of the bus.

MY MOTHER WAS having a difficult time deciding
whether to replace the window. It was still a good window,

a large glass square looking out onto the sloping front yard and street. Two double-hung windows on each side were fitted with summer screens, now fuzzy with dust.

"If you were going to change windows, shouldn't you have done it before painting the room?" I asked Alex.

"I can replace windows very cleanly, and I'll touch up afterward," Alex said. After an awkward silence, he added: "It won't cost you anything extra."

When I was eleven, a crow flew into the living room window and killed itself. The window didn't shatter, but the thud was so resounding I heard it from my bedroom and came running downstairs. Pappa went outside and picked up the crow by its feet while I watched through the window. He held the carcass up to me triumphantly as though he had shot the bird himself. The feathers left a greasy smear on the glass.

"You have to consider how the old window will look in a new room," Alex said, making a sweeping gesture toward the floor.

My mother nodded, her hands gripping her waist. She was wearing a blue sweatsuit, her working uniform. Her eyes watched the contractor's hands.

"We'll be putting in beautiful oak. Long, thin slats. Think of the striped movement toward the fireplace."

"I see."

"I think you need a simpler window. There will be too much going on otherwise. Too many blocks here"—he gestured towards the window—"and strips." He pointed to the floor and looked at me. "Do you understand what I'm talking about?"

"I haven't a clue," I replied.

Alex turned and began measuring the window. He hummed, pausing for a moment to turn his painter's cap backward on his head. There was a white outline on the back pocket of his jeans where he kept a pack of cigarettes.

"You don't need a new window," I whispered to my mother as we watched. She had a stern look on her face, and her glassy eyes told me her mind was occupied.

"Alex has some good points, about that movement to the fireplace," she murmured.

Alex continued to measure, scribbling numbers with a pen on his palm. I turned my back toward him and hovered over my mother. "He's not an interior designer," I whispered. "He just wants to sell you a window."

She cupped her chin in her hand and shook her head. "I'm sure he's just concerned about everything looking nice," she replied.

When it came to strangers, my mother always gave them the benefit of the doubt. On Halloween, teenagers knocking down mailboxes, including ours, were young at heart. The garbage collectors who left trash scattered on our driveway were in a hurry, trying to be efficient. She even forgave the raccoons who spread our milk cartons and tuna-fish cans further down the street, saying man had tampered with the delicate ecosystem.

"He's running a business, plain and simple," I said. "There's nothing artistic about it."

My mother's face loosened slightly. Her jaw, which was usually firmly clamped under her mouth, slipped.

"I know about business," she said, blinking. She smoothed her sweatshirt over her stomach. "I may not have a snappy tongue like you, but I know about business," she continued. Then she called out: "Alex!"

The contractor turned to face us, a pen dangling from his mouth. His stomach was flat, almost sunken. Oily fingerprints dotted the windowpane.

"Alex, you may be right, in some ways." My mother's voice wobbled, and she coughed to steady it. "A new window would be lovely. Very lovely. But I am one who believes that you have to mix old and new."

Alex nodded solemnly and released the end of the measuring tape. The thin, metallic strip snapped back into its holder like a frog's tongue after clinching a fly. "Is it the money?" he asked, glancing at me.

My mother laughed lightly. "Of course not. It's simply a question of history. Without that window, it's as if we were never here."

"I understand," he said, sighing.

"So, no new window."

"Got it. No window, Mrs. Shimoda."

"By the way." My mother again put her hand to her chin. "Will you be using tongue-and-grooved boards?"

Alex looked startled. "Why, yes, Mrs. Shimoda. Unless, of course, you'd like something else."

"Please, call me Hanako."

My mother stared intently at the floor while Alex smiled widely. "Hanako," he repeated, slowly. "That's a beautiful name. What does it mean?"

"*Hana* means flower. *Ko* means child."

Alex's eyebrows climbed skyward. "Flower child? Like a hippie girl from the sixties?" He snapped his fingers and swiveled his hips in a vague dance.

My mother tittered, her hands covering her laughing mouth. "Heavens, no! It's a very traditional, romantic name in Japanese, I suppose like Elizabeth or Catherine in English. I had a romantic mother."

"So did I," said Alex, feet planted firmly apart, his freighted tool belt slung low on his hips like a cowboy's holster. "Alex is short for Alexander."

After an awkward moment, they both laughed, Alex with an open mouth and his head thrown back, while my mother giggled and watched.

BEN'S FRIENDS WERE creative and artistic, talking about the latest Wim Wenders film or Don DeLillo book, their hair studiedly unkempt. I was fascinated by them, a group of people with opinions they had to shout out in order to be heard above the others. Their ideas and attitudes were already tightly woven together; mine were vague and unformed by comparison. In their presence, I would cower near Ben as if he were a shield.

One day, during a break between classes, I sat on the arts quad watching the Frisbees sailing in the air, the dogs chasing the Frisbees, the boys applauding their dogs. A familiar confidence flowed through me as I pulled out a pad and a pencil; I knew I could draw what I saw and draw it well. I did a simple contour drawing and felt pleased at my efforts.

When I showed Ben the sketch, he glanced at it and returned it to me.

"Very nice," he said.

"Thanks," I replied, my face hot with embarrassment. I felt silly for wanting his praise, for offering up the sketch like a child. I stuffed the drawing into my backpack.

"You don't have to prove to me that you can draw," he said.

I shrugged.

"But an occasional doodle doesn't mean much," he added without a trace of dismissiveness or judgment in his voice.

"What's that supposed to mean?" I asked, fighting to loosen the tightness in my throat.

"I'm just saying that being talented doesn't mean much, doesn't mean anything. What matters is that you care."

• • •

I CALLED CHARLOTTE to tell her Alex had painted over the height wall.

"Oh, we should have preserved that!" she said. "We could have covered it with glass and framed it, or something."

"Well, it's gone."

"How's everything else?" she asked.

"Good," I replied. "Mom's getting along pretty well with the contractor."

"Really? I like hearing that. That's nice."

I listened to her chew gum for a few moments.

"So when are you going to get out of there?" Charlotte asked.

"I kind of feel like I should stick around for a while. Don't you ever feel guilty about moving to Chicago? Like you've deserted her or something?"

"What, is something wrong with Mom?" she asked, her words coming out in a rush.

"No. I'm just curious."

Charlotte sighed. "Well, I personally don't think there's any reason for us to feel guilty." She paused for a moment, as if watching something pass by her window. "First of all, she's healthy and still relatively young. Secondly, she left her mother behind in Sado to come to America. You realize that, don't you? If she felt free enough to do that, I should feel free enough to come to Chicago."

"I suppose you're right."

We both fell silent, and I looked out Pierre's window, watching a young man glide down the street on his bicycle, back upright, leisurely putting on riding gloves as if sitting in the back of a car. I thought about how, on some Sundays while growing up, I'd peer into the coming week and see only bleakness. Standing in the living room, gazing over my father napping on the couch and through the front picture window, I'd look out onto the street, only slightly grayer than the sky: There would be some movement—a leaf turning, a bird or plane skimming the air —but otherwise the stillness was overwhelmingly complete. I imagined the mundane chores people were performing, hidden in their silent houses: washing dishes, cleaning out closets. It seemed that one Sunday moment, waiting for another week to begin, summed up their whole lives.

And standing there, looking out the window, my father exhaling deeply on the sofa, my mother puttering around in the kitchen, I'd feel as distant from my family as from the strangers living across the street. It never occurred to me then that my father and mother, too, could be experiencing something private, the vast past of their lives hurtling through their minds and distilling into that one Sunday afternoon.

"Maybe she doesn't see the world the way I imagine," I told Charlotte. "It would be nice to think so."

• • •

I CALLED UP the Better Business Bureau, but found no one had filed any complaints against Alex. "That doesn't necessarily mean anything, honey," the secretary told me.

"Really?" I said, listening to her long nails tapping on a keyboard.

"You should see what happened to my house when I renovated," she continued, her voice tangy and eager. "Hired a guy with solid credentials, great references, nice, smooth personality. After he finished, there was a heavy rain and *splosh!* Got a hole in my roof the size of Toledo. And I couldn't track down Nicky for the life of me. He's probably running a scam in Connecticut or something. If you hear the name Nicky Flint, I suggest you vamoose in the other direction."

ALEX DISCOVERED DIRTY magazines in my brother's room, termites in the garage walls, four-year-old canned soups in the hall closet. He brought his discoveries to our attention in a matter-of-fact way, like a cat depositing a dead mouse on the doorstep. "You're paying me to make your home my business," he'd say, but I was never sure how much he came across by accident or how much was simply a result of snooping.

Then, one evening as I searched my drawers for a pen, I noticed that my old Japanese textbooks were missing. Although I hadn't opened them since we stopped going to

Japanese school, they had always been in the bottom
drawer of my desk.

I found my mother in the kitchen, rearranging her
cookbooks on the counter.

"What happened to my Japanese books?" I asked.

"Oh, I gave them to Alex," my mother said, opening a
file of old recipes. "He's interested in picking up a little
Japanese."

She laughed, holding up a few index cards that looked
toasted. "Remember when I was going through my sauer-
braten and brandied-fruit phase?" she asked.

"You gave my books to Alex?" I said, my voice rising
and suddenly querulous. "Why didn't you ask me? Those
books are a part of my childhood. I want to keep them."

My mother continued to go through the yellowed cards.
"Neither you nor Charlotte cared much for that school. I
thought you'd be glad to put them to good use."

"But the books are mine. Since when is Alex so interested in studying Japanese anyway? And why are his little
interests so important to you? He acts like he owns the
place. And you're letting him."

"Certainly not."

"Well, you're letting him use the car."

"I don't see anything wrong with that," my mother
replied. She riffled through *The Joy of Cooking* and plied
apart two pages stuck together with a brown splotch of
dried sauce. "His truck's in the garage, getting the trans-

mission fixed. There's nothing wrong with helping him out," she added.

My mother trusted everybody. She never locked doors or asked neighbors to keep an eye on the house when she was away. Sleeping alone with an acre of dark, spiky woods out back had never worried her. In the mornings she dressed with the windows wide open.

"I just don't want Alex to start feeling like he's got the upper hand in this house," I said. The tiles chilled my bare feet. "It's your house and I don't think he's treating it seriously," I added.

My mother was silent, using a dishrag to wipe away a cobweb on a cookbook before lining it up with the others. She was too proud to be truthful. It was easy for her to feel angry and resentful toward my father, but she would never acknowledge it if someone else insulted or offended her, or treated her badly.

"I mean, look here." I walked to the stove, pointing to the imported blue ceramic tile on the wall above the burners.

"This is obviously crooked, Mom. Lining up tile is a skill that Alex should have mastered by now."

My mother looked at me blankly.

"How much was this tile?" I asked.

"Hand-painted. Twenty dollars apiece," my mother replied. "And worth every penny."

"You should ask Alex to do this over again," I told her. I

slid into a kitchen chair, flushed and empowered by the sternness of my own words.

"Frankly, I think the tiles look quaint," my mother said evenly. "Like we were living in the Italian countryside."

"Oh please. I suppose the Italians have holes in the floor, too." I pointed to two holes by the floor-to-ceiling windows where a radiator had been removed.

"Alex is aware of those holes. He has momentum now, so he thought it would be best to move on to other rooms. He'll fix all that soon enough."

I rested my chin on the palms of my hands, my elbows propped up on the kitchen table, and rubbed my temples. "Who referred Alex to you?" I asked.

"He left his business card in my mailbox," my mother replied.

I imagined Alex rambling around in his old truck, wheezing to a stop at every mailbox on the street. "Great," I muttered.

"I don't understand you." My mother began slapping cookbooks, one at a time, up against each other into a row. "You and Charlotte have been pushing me for so long to renovate, to cleanse the house of Pappa's things, to start a new life. Now that I have, you are so unsatisfied."

"Well, I was hoping you'd pick a Japanese contractor. Someone you could deal with more easily, on your own terms."

"You don't think I can deal with Alex?"

"No," I replied.

My mother clasped her hands together, and opened her eyes so wide that the irises were surrounded by whites, like two brown islands.

"Then by all means, leave," she said.

There was a moment of sudden silence. "That's fine with me," I replied, standing up and pushing my chair in toward the table. The chair stuttered, and I saw with angry satisfaction that I had left pale scuff marks on the new floor.

"Fine," my mother said curtly, turning her attention back to the cookbooks.

I WENT OUTSIDE, slamming the front door shut behind me. From the corner of my eye I could see Alex at the picture window, his arms outstretched above him, a puzzled look on his face. I took the porch steps in twos and strode down the front lawn.

When I was a very little child, I once headed down the driveway with my mother to pick up the mail. The day was fine and sunny, and I had eagerly embarked on our adventure.

I was holding my mother's hand, and we approached the driveway's end, where our white mailbox stood. I looked out across the street to our neighbor's white house, with their big white- and pink-flowered trees, as my mother opened the mailbox with its creaky whine and retrieved the mail. For most of my brief life, my mother had been more a hand to me than a person.

There, at the bottom of the driveway, I felt my mother's hand loosen around mine. And I turned to see her heading quickly back up toward the house. She was wearing a bright blue shirt. For a moment, standing by myself at the edge of the driveway where the world began, I felt exhilarated. But then quickly, I was flooded with anxiety and worry about how I would return home.

Many years later, when I watched a film of this incident, I could see how unaware I was of my father kneeling in the grass in the front yard, or of my mother at the top of the driveway, coaxing me to walk up the hill. All I recalled was being stranded alone at the bottom of the driveway and not being able to hear or see anybody.

I headed down the hill past the Williamses, a black family with a pool and a shriveled bulldog, who lived diagonally from us; past two Chinese families with kids who lit firecrackers at night; past a couple from Chile who had painted their house both yellow and purple. Of the sixteen families on the small street, only the Herberts and the O'Briens were white.

It was dusk, and the black trees mixed with the plum sky like drops of ink in a glass of water. I turned left at the end of our street and began up a steep hill, stretching the muscles in my calves with each step. Two cars rushed by. I walked quickly, on the left side of the road, arms pumping at my sides, although my energy began to lessen as I made my way up the incline, my anger giving way to anxiety.

My initial impulse was to take the next train into the city and stay with Leilani, my freshman-year roommate. Then maybe I'd go visit Charlotte in Chicago. But what would I do in Chicago? And I wasn't sure I could endure an inevitable "shape up or ship out" talk from my sister.

A car honked from behind and pulled up slowly to my right side. I stared steadily ahead, recognizing the refrigerator yellow of my mother's Volvo.

"Come back," Alex called out through the driver's window. He drove uneasily, turning his head quickly toward me, and then back to the windshield. "Your mother really wants you home," he added.

"How do you know what my mother thinks?" I hissed. The hill had steepened considerably and the car jerked forward in little spurts.

"It doesn't take a genius to see that she's lonely," Alex said.

Headlights appeared at the hill's crest, and Alex pulled the Volvo over to let the car pass between us.

"I'm not a bad guy," he added, nearing me and almost nudging my hip with the car door.

"You're a bad driver," I told him.

Alex pulled away again to avoid a fallen branch lying in the street. "From your point of view, I can't do anything right," he added, veering toward me again as we reached the top of the hill.

"I have high standards," I said.

"Listen. I'm just trying to do my job, and your mother is happy with me."

"You're pushing her to do more than she needs to with the house."

"Me? She's the one, pushing me to get the place ready for Luciano."

I stopped walking. The wind blew through the brittle leaves of a dead tree branch over my head.

"Luciano?" I asked.

Alex put the car into park and flicked on the hazards with relief. "He's coming to visit," he said.

"Luciano Pavarotti is coming to see us?"

Alex nodded. "Sometime soon. That's why she's in such a hurry to get the house done."

I walked around the front of the car and opened the front passenger door. "Home," I ordered, sliding into the seat. I stared through the dark windshield.

Alex grimaced while looking into the rearview mirror, then pulled a sloppy U-turn, leaving tracks on someone's lawn.

FOUR

My mother was sitting in the kitchen with her back to the door, her feet propped up on a nearby chair. From the reflection in the window I could see that her face bore a completely empty expression, her eyes focused on the night's blackness, her mouth compressed into a tight line. She always looked this way when deep in thought, her face a still pool, never revealing what lurked beneath. Her feet, however, were busy, one big toe trying valiantly to hook itself around the other.

"So what's this about Pavarotti?" I asked, feeling my cheeks flush.

My mother turned in her chair and looked up at me. "That was a short trip," she remarked.

"Alex tells me Pavarotti's coming over," I said.

"Oh! I wanted it to be a surprise."

"It's true?"

"Yes. Indeed." My mother laughed, covering her mouth with her hand. "I thought it would be nice for you to come home from work one day and see Luciano sitting here in my beautiful kitchen."

"Come on. Pavarotti?"

"Yes, Pavarotti. Remember that evening when Mrs. Murata and I met Luciano in his dressing room?" My mother lowered her voice to a whisper. "While we were chatting he mentioned he was appearing at a charity performance in Purchase. I told him I lived close by."

She sighed deeply, her shoulders rising and falling with her breath. "He said he'd visit on the way back to New York City," she added, her voice disappearing as she spoke until she simply mouthed the word *city*.

"That's it? Oh God, I thought you were serious," I said, and started to laugh.

"I am serious, he's coming," my mother replied, her voice full again, but slightly indignant. She blinked at me.

"Oh, Mom."

"Why shouldn't he? He said he would. You weren't there."

"Think about it. This is Pleasant Springs. Why would he come here?"

"I can talk to Luciano about music," my mother said. "Not everyone can offer that kind of knowledge."

"There are plenty of people he can talk to about music.

I think Pavarotti was probably just being polite, making conversation."

My mother sniffed. "Luciano has more integrity than that," she said.

"What exactly did he say that night?"

"If I recall correctly, he said 'Madame Shimoda, I would love to come to your house and sing a duet.'"

"You told him the story about your brother?"

My mother nodded. "He seemed very touched by it. Mrs. Murata said his eyes were nearly filling with tears."

"And this renovation is because of him?"

"The performance is in two months. For now, I'm just going to do the rooms he might see." She closed her eyes and lifted her chin. "The kitchen and the living room. And of course, the bathroom."

I folded my hands in front of me, my arms and upper chest leaning on the table. "There's a big difference between saying 'would love to' and 'will,'" I said gently.

My mother shook her head vigorously. "He's coming, believe me. I could tell by the tone of his voice."

DESPITE HER BELIEF that the world's most famous opera singer was coming to visit, my mother continued to act perfectly normally. I tried to spot subtle signs of some inner turmoil, or a secret smile that indicated this was all a joke between Alex and her, but there was neither. The morning after her confession, she began cleaning the bottom of the oven with cheerful vigor, scrubbing a solid puddle of burnt melted cheese with a bristly brush, her small hands encased in yellow rubber gloves.

"I'm so excited about all this," she said, pausing to spray more oven cleaner.

I looked at her cautiously as I measured new shelf paper to lay in a cupboard. "I hope you're not getting your hopes up too high."

"It's too late! My hopes are sky-high!" my mother exclaimed, scrubbing enthusiastically until the cheese disintegrated into foamy flecks, which she scraped up into her palms and threw atop the garbage.

"Isn't that oven self-cleaning?" I asked.

"So they say. But it's such a small spot, and I have so much energy today!"

After closing the oven door, my mother peeled off her rubber gloves and tossed them in the sink, then opened all the windows, letting in the green scent of cut grass.

LATER THAT MORNING, I found her at the kitchen table, a stack of blank stationery in front of her, a fountain pen in her hand.

She turned to me. "I'm writing him a letter," she said. "In English or Italian, this is a problem."

"What's the problem?" I asked.

"Do you think he's able to easily read a letter in English?"

"I'd think so. He must get a lot of his fan mail in English."

My mother snorted. "This is not a fan letter! This is a formal greeting. Perhaps I will write it in Italian. It will make him feel comfortable and at ease."

"Oh yeah? How easy is your Italian to read?"

She ignored me and started to write. *"Non ho parole a esprimere il giubilo ch'io provo,"* she said out loud. "Is that right?"

I rolled my eyes.

My mother chuckled. "Actually, I'm stealing a few words from Nemorino in *L'elisir d'amore.* You know the character of Nemorino, don't you? I wonder if Pavarotti'll notice."

"What are you writing?"

"'I cannot put into words the joy I feel,'" my mother said.

"Isn't that a little melodramatic?" I asked.

"Perhaps I will quote Nemorino when he gets the elixir. 'You fill my breast with so much joy!' *'Di tanta gioia già mi colmi il petto!'"*

She paused, opening a tin of biscotti. "I'm not so sure about the spelling, though. I wish Pierre were here," she said, gnawing at the end of a cookie. "His Italian is so good."

"Hmmmm."

"Fortunately, I just ordered new stationery with my initials on the top. The paper is delicately outlined in gold. Do you like it?"

"Where are you going to send it?"

"To the Met, of course. I'm certain they'll get the letter to him. I want Pavarotti to understand how I feel. I want him to know that *il tuo viso ho sculto in petto*. His image is engraved on my heart.

"I need something to stimulate my brain," she said, and got up to clear away a stack of old telephone books and mail from the counter. She lifted an espresso machine from the floor. "Would you like some?"

"When did you get that?"

"Last week. In Little Italy," my mother said, pinging the heavy metal of the shiny machine with her fingernail. *"Magnifico."*

My mother plugged the machine in, pulled a bag of ground espresso out of the freezer. She carefully spooned some into the metal espresso scoop and filled the machine from a large plastic bottle of water whose label read *Fiuggi.*

"How I love *caffè*," she told me, hovering by the espresso machine, watching as a tiny, dark stream appeared and dribbled into her white cup.

"This is the best kind. It has *selezione elettronica dei grani di caffè difettosi,*" she added.

"What does that mean?" I asked.

"Electronic detection of defective coffee beans," she replied, gliding to the refrigerator to retrieve a small dish of slivered lemon peel. "It means they pick out the low-quality beans so only the best are left."

She brought the cup back to the table and bent over the coffee, inhaling deeply.

"The Italians understand life," she said, seating herself. She held a piece of peel with both hands over the cup and twisted it briskly, to no apparent effect. "They understand music, they understand food, they understand coffee. What more can there be?"

She rubbed the peel briskly around the cup's rim before taking a sip.

"*Gustosissimo,*" she said, kissing her fingertips.

T H E   S I N G E R S   C A M E armed with folders of sheet music and canvas tote bags filled with cassette tapes, boxes of throat lozenges, and packets of chamomile tea. Everyone kissed upon greeting, lips barely grazing cheeks. There was a heady, nervous energy in the air, as in a stable of race-horses.

"This room looks like a war zone!" exclaimed Gisela, a lush, voluptuous woman in her early fifties, as she stepped over a roll of carpet that Alex had torn up. The floor's surface was an uneven, sickly yellow. Our furniture was mostly piled in the dining room, obstructing light. The living room was dark, mottled, and vulnerable, as if ravaged by illness.

"Oh, we're fixing it up," my mother replied cheerfully. "We've been quite busy here."

"You look happy, Hanako," Gisela said, smiling gently.

Her soft, white face still retained traces of the beauty from her youth: a full, pink mouth, arched eyebrows, and small, shell-like ears. She had studied at Juilliard and (so the story goes) was destined for fame and the Metropolitan Opera before a weakness for men and nightlife took a toll on her voice and reputation. She still sang in local productions, most recently as a slightly matronly Madame Butterfly, but teaching paid the bills. My mother had met the singers in a continuing-education class taught by Gisela at a nearby college.

"Did anyone see Pavarotti in his new role?" Bernard asked, stirring sugar into his coffee with a spoon. He shook his head when I offered him some milk. "Dairy coats the vocal cords," he murmured, pinching his Adam's apple.

Bernard was Italian, married to Inge, who was Swedish. He sang, she did not, but they both attended the group meetings. "In *Andrea Chénier*." Bernard tapped the spoon on the cup's edge. "He made a few mistakes but his voice was apparently formidable. At least according to the *New York Times*."

Gisela laughed, her throaty exhalation vibrating deep in her throat. "Formidable or not, that's a man in crisis, I tell you. And I've known many a man in crisis."

"Speaking of men in crisis, I found a condom in my son's jacket yesterday," said Lynne, a single working mother who sang a lot of Billie Holiday. "He's thirteen, for God's sake."

As the conversation waned, Gisela walked to the front of

the living room and positioned herself beside the card table my mother had put there. She inserted a cassette into a tape player and, after clearing her throat, pressed the play button with a manicured fingernail.

The taped piano accompaniment wavered at first, as if warped by damp weather, but steadied as Gisela began to sing. Her voice was high, at times almost piercing, but its fullness was striking, filling every corner of the house with sound. She held the last note so fiercely, her eyes blazing, her palms turned upward and rising in the air as if asking us all to rise, that I imagined the glass windows would shatter.

"Bravo!" yelled Bernard, clapping furiously.

"Simply wonderful!" my mother exclaimed. "Wonderful."

Gisela bowed her head and curtsied slightly before walking back to her seat.

Bernard shook his head. "The way you sing," he said. "It's a gift."

"A gift?" Gisela snapped her head toward Bernard, as if he had just insulted her. "Do you know why I sing like that?" she asked. "I sing like that because I have nothing else in my life. My voice is my life. Without it, I have nothing."

Her words echoed in the room, the air now thin and empty. Gisela blushed, but shook her carefully set hair and continued to speak. "I know the value of my voice. I exercise and treasure it, I pour everything I have into it. If you're talking gifts, you're talking about Pavarotti. He's so talented, but always so distracted."

My mother was beaming. "I must tell you all something," she whispered.

The four heads swiveled in her direction.

"Because you are all such good musical friends, I must tell you a secret," my mother continued, smiling broadly. "Pavarotti is coming to my house."

"Here?" Gisela's face flushed. "Pavarotti's coming here?"

My mother closed her eyes and nodded curtly. "After he performs at a charity concert at Purchase. I met him a few weeks ago, and he told me he'll be coming by. That's why I'm fixing the house."

Bernard's mouth hung slightly open. He raised his coffee cup to his mouth but returned it to its saucer without taking a sip. "Are you two friends?" he asked.

My mother shook her head. "Not at all," she trilled quickly, her voice losing some of its strength.

"And you're certain he's coming here?" Bernard asked, more softly.

"Oh, yes. Of course. I have a good feeling about us. We may not be friends now, but we will become so, I am certain, before long."

There was an uneasy silence, and I watched the smile on my mother's face grow strained.

"Well, this calls for a group sing, in celebration," Gisela suddenly declared, standing with her arms outstretched.

She launched into "Libiamo, ne' lieti calici," the joyous drinking song from *La traviata,* and the rest of the singers immediately joined in, rising to their feet, exuberant, my mother's high voice the loudest of those filling the room.

ONE HOT EVENING in Rome, my father drove for three hours, circling the same rotaries, repeating the same one-way streets, in search of a restaurant in the Fodor's guide. While Charlotte, Pierre, and I groaned in the backseat of the tinny rented car, Pappa drove grimly on, occasionally consulting the map open on my mother's lap. The sun set and the sky darkened. We drove and drove, pausing once for gas, but never asking for directions. As we raced up and down strange streets, my mother remained as committed as my father to finding La Trattoria Luna and eating a plate of their *linguine alla vongole.*

Charlotte was the one who found the restaurant, pointing to a wooden crescent moon, no bigger than a large croissant, hanging over a street corner. The restaurant was on the second floor, and after driving for half an hour more looking for a place to park, we finally made our way up a flight of stairs, so hungry that it didn't matter if the food was good or bad. My parents were both pleased at their conviction, spreading the starched cloth napkins on their laps with calm satisfaction, and they looked at the menus with an easy grace, as if they had just walked up the street and stumbled into the place.

It was with this kind of perseverance that my parents tackled America. Pappa had been sent by a large Japanese company to sell shiny steel subway cars, silvery bullets resistant to graffiti. He plunged into his work, entertaining clients nearly every night of the week. He began to fill out his suits, not only because Western food packed meat onto his thin frame, but because his salary had doubled from what he had been making in Japan. After a rare dinner at home, he'd light a cigar and retreat to his den, happy to work some more.

He struck pay dirt in the early 1980s, and slowly his cars began to replace the old ones in the Metropolitan Transit Authority's lots. Meanwhile, my mother picked up English rapidly, chatting with the postman and bank teller, using every opportunity to learn a new word or utter a new phrase. She took great delight in saying "damn" or even "shit." For a while, they seemed to be enjoying the new lives they had created in America, re-creating themselves in the process.

Then one morning it all changed. I woke up early to finish some homework; Charlotte, back for spring break, was showering, and Pierre was in his room. Pappa, who had just returned the day before from a business trip, was still sleeping.

"What's for breakfast?" I asked.

"I'm still thinking about what to make," my mother replied, tying an apron around her waist.

"Why are you wearing an apron? You never wear aprons in the morning."

My mother looked up at me, her hands pausing at the small of her back. "I don't want to get my clothes dirty," she said.

It took a few moments for her to tie the strings together, but when she finished, she leaned back against the kitchen sink again.

"Do you like the wallpaper?" my mother asked. She crossed her arms over her chest and cocked her head, as if looking at our yellow-flowered paper for the first time.

"I wouldn't pick it myself, but it's O.K.," I answered. I turned in my chair and looked at the paper behind me to see if anything had changed, to see if, perhaps, my mother had wallpapered a wall in the kitchen overnight as a lark. But the old paper, with its yellow flowers outlined in black, was there as always.

We were both silent, my mother with her arms crossed, the apron tightly wound around her waist, while I sat at the empty table. Upstairs, I heard the water stop and the plastic rings of the shower curtain rattling across the metal railing.

"She leaves things in his luggage," my mother said quietly. She began examining the skin on her fair arms, her eyes inspecting the white surface, and then rubbed a patch of rough skin at her elbow with two fingers.

I didn't say anything at first, although I knew whose luggage we were talking about. My father's suitcase, brown leather with a dial lock at the top, was always packed and unpacked by my mother. Her eyes traveled below her arms and now inspected the linoleum.

"A hair clip. Sterling silver."

"Could it have gotten in there accidentally?" I asked.

My mother laughed loudly, the sound erupting from her mouth in short, unnatural bursts. "Between his under-shirts? No, I don't believe so. She wanted me to find it."

"Hey Mom!" Charlotte called from her room. "Do you know where my blue button-up shirt is?"

"I ironed it and put it in your closet," my mother shouted back, her voice even and sure, as if sturdied by Charlotte's question.

"I don't see it," Charlotte yelled. Then her voice trailed off, saying, "Oh, wait a minute. Oh, yeah, sorry. I found it."

My mother began cracking eggs on the side of a frying pan, Charlotte having kick-started her efficient morning routine. I thought about what she had said. It seemed im-possible that something so dramatic and corrupt could occur in our house. I couldn't imagine my father, in his early fifties, acting in a manner that was inviting, enticing to a woman. I tried to picture such a woman talking to my father, laughing, flirting, touching him.

Pappa came down the stairs, showered and shaved, dressed in a starched shirt and ash gray suit. I watched him as he sat down and sipped his coffee. While he drank, his eyes met mine. I continued to stare, trying to detect a flicker of guilt or uncertainty. But he stared firmly back, his head barely moving as he lowered the cup onto its saucer. With his eyes still on me, his face began to lower as well, nearing the plate of fried eggs my mother had put in front of him. Suddenly, he dipped his face toward the eggs and sucked up one of the runny yolks, leaving behind a hollow in the white. Laughing, he looked back to me, pleased at his joke, waiting for my response.

IN THE BEGINNING, Alex was like all the other occasional men who roamed through our house, fixing the washing machine when it didn't spin or tinkering with a dead microwave. His jeans were slick at the seat and the knees, and his workboots made him sound bigger and heavier than he really was.

Only his truck, painted the color of overcooked peas, was peculiar. That faint green, an elegantly tired green, was the color of my mother's wedding kimono. My grandmother had picked the fabric. "She might not have been the best mother, but she was very good with color," my mother said once, when looking at her wedding album years ago. She said the color of the truck convinced her Alex was reliable. Her reasons for coming to conclusions about people were bewildering. Once she told me she married my father because he was the only man in Tokyo she knew who wore a green felt hat.

At first my mother tried treating Alex like an employee,

asking him what time he could be expected the next morning or how much materials would cost. He displayed the appropriate courtesy, nodding gravely at her comments, explaining in detail the types of nails he was using or the brand of cement. But these formalities were soon dropped. Before long, it was as if Alex had always been with us, a curious observer of our lives.

I watched Alex's truck pause at the bottom of our driveway as he downshifted before roaring up the hill to where I was standing. He turned off the engine and burst out of the truck, stamping the driveway with his heavy boots. A smile inched up one side of his face.

"I've got a surprise," he said, wagging a calloused finger at me. The back of his truck was covered with canvas, which he grabbed and tugged off with a flourish. A door, painted a glossy red, lay in the bed like a slab of hard candy.

"Some door, huh?" he said, his right hand gripping his bony hip. "I thought your mother might want something to brighten up the house." Alex reached into the truck's bed and tried out the large brass knocker, which sounded surprisingly solid. "Hey, listen to that." He knocked again. "Sounds like the door to an important house."

"The red's too loud," I said, folding my arms in front of my chest, then unfolding them. I felt uncomfortable enough with our house the way it was, slumped on the side of the street like an old man. There was no need to draw more attention to it.

Alex looked at me and laughed. "Your family could use a little loud."

He grasped the door with his hands and, with startling strength, lifted it out of the truck in one slow, graceful movement, his fingertips pressed white against the lacquered wood. Holding the door to one side like a sign, he headed toward the front of the house. He whistled to a bird that sprang into the overgrown bushes along the path.

"Oops. Got to keep quiet," he whispered over his shoulder.

He climbed to the top of the porch stairs and set the door against the front railing, careful not to scrape the paint. In the extended silence that followed, I examined the gritty stubble on Alex's chin, the wrinkled patches around his eyes, his mouth that drooped to the left.

"I don't like you," I said.

Alex exhaled and patted around his tool belt, searching for a screwdriver. "I know," he answered.

"You're taking advantage of my mother," I added.

He checked the size of the screwdriver he had pulled out from his belt. "I'm not trying to be your father," he said, kneeling by the front door. He looked up at me. "You want to help me out here?" he asked, squinting in the sunlight.

DESPITE MY RESERVATIONS, the door dressed up the house like a slick of bright lipstick on a pale woman's face.

"Why, it's lovely," my mother said, backing down the porch stairs onto the slate walkway. Then she backed up further until she was in the middle of the front yard. Over her blue sweatpants she was wearing a robe I had never seen before, printed with pink and white poppies.

"Simply wonderful!" she exclaimed.

Alex beamed, looking down at his hands as they brushed off his jeans. "Well," my mother said, slowly walking back up the yard, "I certainly hope that our house will match such a door."

"Don't worry, Hanako," Alex said, reaching his arm out to my mother. She hesitated before resting her fingers on his shirtsleeve. "We're going to make your house beautiful," he said, patting her hand.

They walked up the steps and into the house, passing under a cluster of dead moths and spiderwebs that clung to the porch light. I could hear my mother talking about bathroom tile.

MY FATHER'S MOTHER died at my uncle's house in Yokohama when she was eighty-five. The news came suddenly, one morning, from a voice over the phone. Nobody cried. My father made plane reservations to Japan and then the Sunday went on like any other. But the feeling inside our home changed. A weariness descended on my parents; my mother slowly hand-washing her slips in the bathroom sink while Pappa climbed the stairs to his den as if his slippers were heavy as stone. It was as though my grandmother's cigarette smoke had seeped in through the receiver and crept through the house, settling on us like a layer of ash. My parents flew to Japan the next day for the funeral and returned a week later with the same vacant expressions they had worn when they left.

"What did she die of?" I asked my mother the day after she returned. She was hemming a skirt, her needle deftly dipping in and out of the wool, like a jumping fish.

"It's difficult to say," my mother replied, measuring a piece of thread against the length of her arm. "She had cancer and a few other things."

"Like what?"

"Alzheimer's disease."

"She went senile?"

My mother paused, looping a knot in the thread with her fingertips and snipping the tail. "Yes. In the end her senility was very bad."

She resumed hemming, pushing the needle in and out, then pulling the thread through the fabric. "She nearly burnt down your uncle's house with her cigarettes."

"Why didn't they put her in a nursing home?"

"Neither your father nor your uncle would allow that," she said.

My mother turned the skirt right side out and held it up in front of her, examining her stitching. "She was never kind to me, you know," she said. "Whenever I was with her, she made me uncomfortable."

She flipped the skirt inside out again, and rethreaded a needle. My uncle had two children, both slightly younger than me, and their home in Yokohama was much smaller than ours, without a yard or garage. I tried to imagine how they could have all fit with my grandmother but could only picture them crowded together in one room. My mother breathed evenly and continued to sew. Her needle skimmed across the skirt, and I couldn't help but feel her relief in the choices we had made.

WHEN I WENT downstairs to the kitchen the morning after he installed the new door, I found Alex in one of my mother's aprons, flipping pancakes at the new stove. My mother was sitting at the table, facing into the room, the sun from the window throwing light over her shoulders. She sipped coffee from a chipped cup she had bought with my father on a trip to Vienna. A pancake, cut into tiny pieces, sat untouched in front of her.

"Carreras is to be admired, of course, considering his fight against leukemia," my mother said, crossing her arms over her chest.

"Uh-huh," Alex replied, pouring circles of batter onto the pan. He motioned for me to sit down. "I'm making a fresh batch," he said.

"But his voice, like his health, is fragile," my mother continued. She looked at me as I slipped into the seat across from her. "What do you think about José Carreras?" she asked.

"He seems like a nice guy, at least on TV," I said.

"No, no, musically. What do you think of him musically? Alex?"

Alex pulled out a plate warming in the oven and heaped it with pancakes. He paused for a minute, the plate in one hand and a metal spatula in the other. His head was cocked, as if expecting to hear a note.

"Carreras's voice is light, not big enough to fill a large concert hall," he answered. "The quality is tender, which is appealing, but tenderness is not enough to sustain leading parts. For example, Carreras is not ideal as Gustavus III in Verdi's *A Mask Ball*."

I looked at him. "What?"

My mother clapped her hands; Alex threw back his head and laughed. He brought the pancakes to the table.

"Did I sound like an expert, or what?" he asked, wiping his hands on his apron.

"That was very good, Alex, but it's Verdi's *A Masked Ball*, not *A Mask Ball*," my mother said.

"Oh right, *A Masked Ball*." He frowned, setting a plate of steaming pancakes in front of me. "Your mother's teaching me a thing or two," he told me, and returned to the stove, where he poured streams of batter high above the pan.

"Although she never tells me anything about herself," he added.

My mother paused. "What would you want to know?" she asked.

Alex shrugged. "How about something about that island you're from?"

"Oh, heavens. What could you find interesting about that little place?" My mother dumped a spoonful of sugar into her cold coffee, but she smiled as she stirred. "Actually, the history is quite interesting. There were many famous people who were exiled to Sado. Emperors and poets."

"Is that right?" Alex said, turning to face us.

My mother nodded. "So from an outsider's point of view, it's a melancholy place, in many ways. The people on the mainland sing that 'even the birds shun Sado.' To them, the island is dark and forbidding.

"But on the island itself, the perception is much different. The islanders sing, 'The trees and grasses wave toward Sado; isn't Sado a wonderful place?'"

"So nobody can really know what someone else's home is like. Right?" said Alex.

My mother nodded, and smiled. "Yes. A poet named Bashō said a 'Heaven's River' in the sky connected Sado with the mainland. But to be honest, I don't know which end of the river he meant was heaven."

"Heaven's River," Alex repeated. "I like that."

"Amanogawa," my mother said. "It's Japanese for the Milky Way."

Alex leaned his sinewy frame against the stove, crossing one leg over the other. "Amanogawa. You know, since I came here from Athens, what is that, forty-five years now, I've never traveled out of the country. I've barely been out of New York State."

He turned, prompted by a burning smell, and quickly tossed five small pancakes from the pan into a wobbly stack on a plate. "Heaven's River," he said again, turning off the burner. He brought the plate to the table and set it in front of my mother. "I want to go and see it someday," he told her.

FIVE

When I called Charlotte, she was in the middle of an exercise video. "Can I call you back?" she asked, her voice tight with exertion. "I'm just starting to feel the burn."

After hanging up, I waited at the kitchen table, looking out the window at my mother and Alex in the backyard. They were dismantling an old swing my brother had hung from the branches of a tree. Alex was perched precariously atop a ladder, fiddling among the leaves. My mother stood beneath him, a few loosened leaves falling down around her, her lips pursed with concern. Alex continued to tug at the chains, the movement jiggling the ladder. The phone rang.

"So what's up?" Charlotte asked.

"It's about Mom. And the house."

"What about Mom?"

"I'm worried about the contractor she's hired. His work is completely shoddy."

"He's ripping her off?"

"She won't tell me anything about finances. But even I can see he's made mistakes. He completely messed up the living room. He splattered paint all over the carpet, so now Mom says she's going to refinish the floor. He installed a new front door without our asking, and I don't know who's paying for it."

"Did you call the Better Business Bureau?"

"Yes, and they've had no complaints. But that doesn't necessarily mean he's any good."

"Why don't you call another contractor? Ask him what he thinks about the house. Have the guy talk to Mom. Maybe she'll listen to a third party."

I glanced out the window just in time to see Alex tug especially hard at the chain, lose his balance on the ladder, and drop a few rungs before catching himself.

"Oh, God," I said.

"What?"

"He just nearly killed himself. I don't understand why Mom doesn't see him for what he is."

LIKE OUR BRONTË namesakes, Charlotte and I lived in a world within a world. Though separated by seven years, we were in many ways as close as twins. Together we had a sensitivity toward our parents and their moods that bordered on instinct; we could communicate potential tension or conflict by exchanging a simple glance.

I wondered whether that firsthand knowledge of the complexities of marriage was the reason we were both alone. Charlotte was smart and attractive; there was no reason for her to be single other than by choice. And while I dreaded loneliness, my sister was exhilarated by being by herself. I suspected that now, for the first time in her life, she felt unfettered by the burden of others.

DAVID HAVERMEYER WAS in his early forties, short but well built, with the cool, neatly confident demeanor of an airline pilot. His shirtsleeves were rolled to just below his elbows, baring forearms bristling with golden hair. Mrs. O'Brien down the street had gushed about him when I called her for a recommendation. He stood in the middle of our kitchen, having finished inspecting the other rooms in the house. He folded his arms across his chest as his eyes made their way around the room, taking in the stovetop and the crooked tiles behind it, the cupboard doors that didn't quite close, the paint-choked sockets. He turned to me, his eyes observing me in much the same way, as if assessing the way the features fit together on my face.

"May I speak my mind?" David asked.

I nodded, now wishing he hadn't come.

"The man who did this," he said, "shouldn't be in this business. Are you sure he's got a license?"

I nodded vaguely. "I think my mother's looked into that," I replied.

Downstairs, the garage door rumbled open, and I heard a faint thud as my mother shut the car door. A moment later, she trudged slowly up the stairs, loaded with bags of groceries. She paused at the kitchen door when she saw us.

"Hi Mom," I said, waving my hand. David quickly retrieved the bags from my mother as I stood uneasily between them.

"Mom, this is David Havermeyer. He's a contractor who built the addition to the O'Brien house last year."

"I see. How do you do?"

David nodded, depositing the groceries on the kitchen table. "I asked David to take a look at our house," I continued.

"Is that so?" My mother pulled out a carton of milk from a bag and put it in the refrigerator.

"I was worried that Alex wasn't doing such a terrific job, but I wanted to get a professional opinion. Just to make sure."

"I see."

Nobody spoke. David, his eyes moving from me to my mother, hesitated before holding his hands out in front of him, as if ready to catch a ball. "There's a lot I can say," he began.

My mother waved her hand in front of her face. "David, I am sure you are a very good contractor. And my daughter seems very interested in your opinions. But I am confident the renovation is going well, and have no worries. No worries at all, in fact. So feel free to discuss matters, but please excuse me."

She left the room and started up the stairs toward her bedroom. I chased after her.

"Mom!" I whispered loudly. "I think you should listen to this guy."

She turned to me, her eyes wide open and angry, her lips a strained line. "Why are you checking up on Alex?" she asked.

"I don't trust him," I replied. "I'm concerned about you, too."

She snorted a laugh. "What makes you so sure he's honest?" she said, nodding toward the kitchen.

"Well, he came recommended."

"But how do you know he's not eager to criticize Alex so that maybe we'll hire him, instead?"

I paused. "He doesn't seem like the dishonest type," I said. "I can tell by the way he talks."

"You're as bad as I am," my mother said, turning her back toward me and marching into her bedroom.

• • •

ALEX ARRIVED IN a happy mood, whistling and singing what sounded like a Greek melody as he came up the stairs. He opened the refrigerator and was looking for the bag of apples and oranges that he kept there when I heard the doorbell, and through the glass door made out the wilted figure of our former gardener Lou. He stood in profile, his body slumped into a question mark, as if he was not meant to be as tall as he was. My mother had discovered him when his business card arrived in our mailbox announcing the services of "Lou, Gardener Extraordinaire." For two years he mowed our lawn unevenly, pruned the shrubs into amorphous shapes, and fertilized only when something died. It wasn't until Charlotte came up for a weekend and caught him stealing rakes that my mother decided to let him go.

But he kept returning. I suspected my mother had been one of very few regular customers, and somehow he believed that by simply appearing when he used to, he'd blend seamlessly back into our lives. He broke out into a wide grin as I opened the door. "Now there's a sight for sore eyes," he declared loudly. His irises swam behind his thick glasses, and he smelled of fresh dirt and gasoline.

"New frames," I said.

Lou nodded. "When I see better, I work better," he replied.

"Why are you here, Lou? We've gone over this before."

"Grass is looking long," Lou said, lifting his baseball cap

and combing his fingers through whatever hair remained underneath. "Grass doesn't look good when it's so long."

"My mother's not going to change her mind," I said.

Lou checked his watch, and shook his head slowly. "It'll be tight, but I could squeeze in a quick mow now, in between appointments," he said.

His knees were slightly bent, his shoulders hunched, as if straining under the weight of all that had come before. Hours spent under the sun left dark, blurry spots on his skin, and his fingers were curved even when at rest, as if molded to the handle of his lawn mower. He traveled with a whiny mutt in the passenger seat of his truck and a pair of stuffed dice hung from his rearview mirror.

Lou stuck the toe of his mud-encrusted workboot into the open door space. "Something has to be done about that bad-looking grass," he muttered. His boot scraped against the door, sending bits of dried mud falling to the floor. We both stood in silence.

"Hey, watch the door. I just put that in." Alex spoke from behind me, and I heard him walk toward us with long strides, covering the distance between the kitchen and the doorway in about four steps.

"Do you mind?" Alex asked, pointing to Lou's foot.

Lou squinted at Alex, his eyes darting wildly, as if trying to take in all the components of his face.

"The lawn is a mess," he announced, straightening up to his full height, which was a few inches taller than Alex.

"You're the mess," Alex said. "I know about you. Get lost, buddy."

Lou lifted an eyebrow and shifted his weight onto his right foot. "You working for her now?" he asked.

"I said, get lost."

Lou smiled, and started to laugh. He looked at me and jerked his head toward Alex. "You've hired this guy?"

I heard coins jangling in his pocket. Alex wiped his hands on his jeans. "What does it matter?" I asked.

Lou snorted. "After all these years, your mother's my concern, of course. And in this world, you've got to be careful." He shifted his gaze to Alex. "She never asks any questions, does she? How much things cost, what needs to be done." And to me he said, "There are people just waiting to take advantage of a woman like that."

He straightened the cap on his head and looked back at Alex. "Are you treating her right? If not, I'll be coming after you. You can count on that." He shook his head slowly and said, "You just don't know about people," his lips stretched tight across his gums.

Alex and I watched Lou go down the stairs, his boots thumping loosely against the slate. He got into his truck, swatted at his dog, and, after a few stuttering tries, started the engine. A lawn mower jiggled uncertainly in the back as the truck lumbered down our driveway and onto the street. I heard the engine pop somewhere in the distance.

"Well," Alex said, as we returned to the kitchen. "That's that."

I sat down and stared at the white tabletop, listening to Alex as he put on a pot of water to boil and searched the cabinets for a tea bag. I knew that in my mother's village in Japan, doors were always flung open to welcome anyone who might feel like passing through. Fishermen, vegetable vendors, children, dogs, and chickens wandered in and out freely. Plumbers became friends, handymen practically family. But that was a safer place and a safer time.

"IS MRS. HANAKO Shimoda there, please?" the voice over the phone asked.

"Yeah, hold on." I dropped the phone into the lap of a kitchen chair and opened the door to the backyard. My mother was bent over at one corner of the property, a hand on her lower back, the other prodding the ground with a finger. The leaves of a maple tree fluttered over her, the tree's branches reaching in four directions like street signs. A hot sun baked the entire yard.

"Telephone," I called out.

"Somebody ate the tomato tree I planted yesterday," she announced, standing, brushing her hands on her pants. "Alex was right. I do need fencing after all."

"It's the telephone."

"Coming."

My mother rushed across the yard, as light on her feet

as a little dog. Where she was raised, her family grew everything from the pumpkin they stewed with soy sauce and sugar to the giant radishes they pickled and ate with rice. But she'd never done more than sprout an avocado pit in a glass by the kitchen sink.

She bounded up the back-porch stairs, huffing slightly, and rubbed her hands together when she got into the kitchen.

"Such a lovely day," she said, taking the phone. "Hello?" she said in her happy voice, the word coming out more like "Hellew?"

I pulled a carton of orange juice from the refrigerator and poured a glass. My mother motioned for me to pour one for her, too.

"Yes, speaking. Yes. Oh, my."

I handed her the glass, and she brought it to her lips but lowered it before drinking.

"How kind. How wonderful. Simply wonderful. It will be a great pleasure. Please give my best regards to Mr. Pavarotti. Yes, thank you very much for calling."

She hung up the phone softly, downed the entire glass, placed it noiselessly on the table and burst into song.

"'Come, my dear treasure! I'll change your fate,'" she sang, slapping her thigh. Barely able to contain herself, she shook her head and flapped her hands in the air, as if drying polish on her fingernails.

"Ha!" she exclaimed. "My ticket will be waiting for me

at the box office. An orchestra seat. See?" She swung at the air in triumph, as if giving an invisible chin a solid punch. "Pavarotti remembered. He's coming to my house. He's definitely coming!"

MANY EVENTS IN my father's life occurred out of my sight, in hotel rooms or offices, and involved people I didn't know. Even when he was at home, he retreated deep within himself, to his den, his presence reduced to a bar of dim light under his door. I'd press my ear to the wood and make out the occasional crackle of paper or a deep exhalation as he smoked. After his mother died, my mother would tell me Pappa had grown proud, thought he was too Western for her, believed he had outgrown us. "You wouldn't believe the things he says to me," she'd say, and, in fact, I couldn't as they came from my mother's lips, anger shaking her voice. "He said to me, 'Look, I can get an American woman.' Can you believe that? How can he say that to me? I should just go back to Japan. How would that be? Bringing us here, to America, and us returning without him. How would that look to everyone?"

My parents would fight after I had gone to bed, Charlotte in her room and me in mine, both of us pretending to be asleep as we listened to muffled shouts downstairs. My mother's high shrieks contrasted with the low growls of my father. Pierre was closer to them, one floor below our room and one floor above the kitchen. I wondered what he could hear, hoping he didn't know enough Japanese to make out what was being said.

The explosive nights were followed by quiet mornings of coffee and eggs. Occasionally, my mother would greet Charlotte and me with a brief, terse synopsis of what had been said the night before. She barely ate, existing only on coffee and Japanese tea. Pierre practically lived in his room. Pappa never explained his side, but his silence was almost a relief compared with my mother's emotional volubility.

When my mother was at her most fragile point, crying and alone, her family and childhood friends thousands of miles away, my instinctive sympathy made me believe that misfortune, with the encompassing force of a natural disaster, had ambushed her.

She had always operated from the vantage point of the privileged class, something she reveled in. When she recounted stories of her youth, growing up wealthy in a small fishing village, she made little attempt to disguise the joy she felt then at being elite.

But wealth muddles destiny. After the war, my mother's family was stripped of most of their assets, and none of my mother's siblings were able to recreate the family's past grandeur. There have been squabbles about how property should be divided, further eroding the dignity of the family legacy. The feeling surrounding the family now is one of melancholy, of greatness gone. My mother's marriage to my father gave her another brief surge to the top. But her husband's success, large in material terms, never surpassed the glory of her youth—something that chafed at him.

Now I can see her life as the result of a simple series of choices: to marry my father, to agree to move to America, to remain with him when he decided to stay. In her fifties, with my father gone, only her sense of entitlement remains.

ONE EARLY MORNING when I was eight years old, I found my mother on the floor of the hallway bathroom. From my bedroom, I had seen that the light was on. I peeked inside and saw her asleep on the pale gray tile, curled around the toilet. She was wearing a white flimsy nightgown, and her limbs were strangely askew, like those of a sleeping child. I stood at the doorway for a moment, mesmerized by the glowing peach walls and this apparition, looking more like a wounded fairy princess than my mother.

Over breakfast, she told me she had spent the better part of the night throwing up. "Your papa and I ate raw oysters at a party last night," she said weakly, her face a bluish white. For some reason, Pappa escaped unscathed and slept until noon.

When I was in middle school, my mother inexplicably covered the bathroom's peach walls with wallpaper, patterned with pink, white, and blue geometric shapes that gave me a headache if I sat on the toilet too long.

But as I sat on the toilet seat, now, watching Alex scrutinize the bathroom, I suddenly became frightened by the changes I had demanded.

"Well, this wallpaper all has to come down," Alex announced, pointing to the corners of the room, where the paper had started to curl.

"Of course," my mother replied. She opened one of the bathroom drawers and began removing its contents: rusted razors, a tube of hair cream, frayed toothbrushes, an old hairpiece she used to pin on as a bun when going to parties. She tossed the items onto the counter as Alex continued speaking.

"Bathrooms are funny," he remarked, leaning toward the mirror and adjusting the part in his hair with a fingernail. "They're supposed to be private places, but people do them up. You wouldn't believe some of the bathrooms I've worked on. Waterfalls and fourteen-karat-gold faucets."

My mother nodded, staring at the countertop, absentmindedly fingering the misshapen hairpiece. Then, as though awakened, she suddenly snatched it from the counter and crammed it into her pants pocket.

Alex bent over the tub. The faucet leaked in big drips, leaving a rust-colored stain above the drain. The grout was deeply mildewed. He tried the shower, which released a fine, gossamer spray.

"Should we concern ourselves with this right now?"

Alex asked, his voice echoing in the tub. "I mean it's not like Luciano is actually going to take a bath. Not unless you're really lucky."

My mother laughed delightedly. "What a thought!" she exclaimed. "I'd have to get a bigger tub!"

"This is ridiculous," I said, rising from the toilet seat. "You're both acting ridiculous."

My mother shot me a look. "You're being very rude."

"Rude? You two are embarrassing." Alex looked up from the tub. "It's embarrassing," I told him.

My mother lunged and slapped my shoulder, as if aiming for a fly. "Shush!" she said.

I left the bathroom and vaulted instinctively up the stairs to my room, slamming the door closed. Moments later, my mother spoke to me through my door. "Please apologize to Alex," she said.

I was lying on my stomach on the bare mattress, the first time I had been in my own bed since coming back home. "No!" I called out, watching a wasp bounce off the window screen. I lifted my head from the pillow, trying to hear her.

"Alex is a good man, please believe me," she said. "He's not a *minaccia*."

I rolled out of bed and opened the door so quickly that she jumped back in surprise. "It's all wrong, can't you see that? And cut it out with the Italian, will you?"

We stared at each other for a few seconds, my mother's gaze unflinching.

"Why can't you believe something good can happen?" she asked. She stood with her legs apart, as if ready for me to push her.

"Good things happen to your father," she added.

"God," I said, flopping back on my bed. "Please don't start on that."

"Why not? Why do you accept it when good things happen to him, but fight against something good happening to me?"

She turned and walked heavily down the stairs. A moment later, I heard her speaking to Alex in the bathroom, and from the sound of their voices, they were acting as if nothing had happened at all.

I LAY IN bed for a long time, staring at my ceiling. When Charlotte, Pierre, and I were little, my mother let us paint our rooms whatever color we wanted. The huge range of possibilities paralyzed me, and I only managed to venture a girlish pink. Charlotte, on the other hand, chose bright yellow walls, and matched them with magenta and green curtains. Pierre opted for a matte turquoise and kept his windows bare.

My room was the smallest: a tiny, perfect square the size of a large closet. When I was younger, I found comfort in the pale symmetry of its four walls, a soothing pink sea that enveloped me as soon as I closed the door. Boxes of college textbooks and term papers took up much of the room now, along with clothes not worn since high school. But as I lay there, I began to sense the calm that the room had given me as a child.

My mother never said she wanted her children to stay close by. Even when she was at her most depressed, she insisted she didn't want to be a burden on her children. But a sense of obligation drew me back home. Now I wasn't sure if it was generated by my mother, or if I used her as an excuse to disguise my own lack of direction.

I examined a beige water stain in one corner of the ceiling and strained to hear snatches of conversation from Alex and my mother. I fell asleep, and when I awoke, the late-afternoon sun cast warm squares of amber light against the wall.

I thought of a game I used to play before getting up for the day. I would lie in my bed and imagine what it would be like to live in somebody else's house, with somebody else's parents, my mind traveling the neighborhood's streets, visiting various households, bland and bizarre.

If I awoke in the yellow colonial around the corner on Blue River Run, Mr. and Mrs. Ericsson would be browning English muffins in their shiny toaster, waiting for the imported coffee dripping into a spotless glass pot. They were a handsome Nordic couple who had mastered a number of activities as a pair: waltzing, tennis, bridge. I remember skating on a crowded lake one winter and everybody, from rowdy hockey players to wobbly children, stopped when the Ericssons took the ice. They skated together in silent unison, as if the same melody played in their heads, their blades cutting perfect curves into the ice. But the Ericssons were Christian Scientists. For them, prayer cured everything. I imagined myself as a teenager being reprimanded by Mr. Ericsson, not for smoking or drinking, but for taking a Tylenol.

Mornings at the Jaffes' would be less ordered. He was a pediatrician, she my piano teacher. They lived in a sleek, modern house, all horizontal lines and glass. Their two daughters smoked French cigarettes and blew smoke out their noses. I envied their moody sophistication and imagined myself with dark circles under my eyes, leading a life far too complicated for a girl my age. But once, during my piano lesson, one of the daughters asked her mother where the bananas were. After a long pause, Mrs. Jaffe closed her eyes and replied tersely: "They're in the oven, and don't ask me why!" Breakfasts there, I thought, would be laced with tension, words filled with unexpected import.

Then, I examined my own home. Having reached through the exercise some small measure of objectivity, I tried to see my family, their life, from the same mental distance as I did the Ericssons or the Jaffes.

The house, pink, an early 1950s split ranch, ordinary to me; the father, brainy, good-looking, impatient, prone to dark moods; the mother, a music lover, an accomplished cook, proud, sometimes unrealistic, and likely, at inappropriate moments, to break out in spontaneous song.

Both parents are emotionally opaque to their neighbors, even to themselves and their children.

And then I pictured the children: my sister, Charlotte, standing in a red business suit, clutching a Coach bag, and pointing out to me her matching shoes. She was, I thought, a young woman intent on living the bright, shiny life of television shows. My brother, Pierre, wearing the sparse stubble of an affected beard, a boy who left home to reinvent himself. And me, a frowning girl, rushing because she's late for an appointment that doesn't matter anyway, stray strands of hair in her eyes, her cheekbones less high and sharp than if her last name had been Ericsson. She's sleeping in the same small room she grew up in, with its pink walls and bay window overlooking the backyard. She feels a kind of comforting familiarity being home, but it's an odd, skewed sensation, like wearing an old pair of somebody else's shoes.

"The ground's too hard," I heard my mother's protesting voice say distinctly from outside. I got out of bed to peer out my window. My mother and Alex were crossing the backyard, their customary laughing and joking gone.

Alex was carrying an old garden shovel, and they stopped at the border of the backyard where the woods began. I heard the shovel scrape on stone. Alex levered a rock out of the ground and quickly opened a small hole in the dark earth. My mother watched, and as she turned slightly, I saw she was holding the wooden box with Giuseppe's ashes. It was quite a large box. Was it because Giuseppe was severely overweight when we put him to sleep, since my mother had insisted on feeding him manicotti and braised celery for the last three years of his life?

She stood by the hole in silence. Alex finished and leaned against the shovel, watching her while the weakening sun cut through the trees. Finally, she squatted and placed the box in the ground. She remained there kneeling, her blue sweatshirt bright against the dark grass, as Alex gently shoveled dirt to fill the hole. He tamped the loose soil with the back of the shovel. And my mother, her face pale and uplifted, smiled.

SIX

Mariko opened the kitchen door just enough to show her face, wide as a plate, and called: "There's a man at your table!"

I didn't budge from my seat on the counter, and continued to watch Hiro and Tetsu massage oiled stones with the blades of their knives.

"You heard her," Hiro prompted.

I patted my thick patterned obi, searching for my order pad. "It's ten o'clock. Doesn't anybody cook at home anymore?" I said.

"There'll be a lot more tomorrow," Hiro said, pursing his lips, making his long, thin mustache move. "And the day after that. One night, before I went to sleep, I tried to figure out how many people I had served since starting here."

He stood silently for a moment, feeling his blade with a

wet, pink finger. I could hear cold water dripping from the faucet into an empty copper teapot. "I think it was about a hundred thousand," he said. Tetsu laughed loudly and slapped Hiro on the back.

The cavernous dining room was empty, except for Alex, who was sucking on a straw that protruded from the belly of a meditating, ceramic Buddha. He smiled and waved vigorously as I walked toward him.

"Hey, that kimono's mighty cute," he called out.

I approached his table quickly. "What are you doing here?" I asked.

"Don't I even get a hello?" he replied, opening and shutting the miniature blue-paper parasol that came with his cocktail.

I turned and glanced behind me. A busboy came out of the kitchen and I spotted Hiro craning his neck, trying to get a look as the door swung open.

"What are you doing here?" I asked again, passing him a menu.

"I'm here to enjoy Japanese food or, as the Japanese say, 'wa-sho-ku,'" Alex said, enunciating each syllable. When I didn't respond, he cleared his throat and opened the menu, shaped in the silhouette of the farmhouse. "Is the lobster fresh?" he asked.

"Of course it's fresh."

"It won't taste like ammonia or anything?" he said, his eyes following his finger as it went down each column.

The hair at the crown of his head shone platinum in the light. "I'm not crazy about eating shellfish that I can't pick out myself," he added.

I tucked my order pad into my obi with a brisk, crisp movement. Alex looked up, his eyebrows high on his creased forehead. "I was just asking. As a matter of fact, I think I'll have the Shogun Surf and Turf."

"Fine."

Alex leaned back in the upright wooden chair and clasped his hands behind his head. "No nails, huh?"

"What?"

"In the building." Alex pointed to the menu. "Says here it's built without nails."

"Oh, yeah. So the story goes."

"That's quite a feat." His eyes began searching the rafters that crisscrossed the ceiling. "I bet I can find one before the night's out," he said.

"WHO IS THE man?" Hiro asked when I returned to the kitchen. Mariko, who had been noisily washing glasses in the sink, paused, her eyes fixed on the drying rack in front of her.

I shrugged, scrawling down the order on my pad and tearing off the top sheet. I handed it to Hiro. "My mother hired him to work on our house," I replied.

Hiro wrinkled his forehead, holding the paper to the light, trying to make out my handwriting. He squinted, bringing the order closer to his face. "I'll see if I can get him a really good piece of steak," he said.

"Don't bother with too much," I told him, and ladled dressing on a bowl of salad. As Hiro headed to the walk-in refrigerator, I called out, "He's very picky about shellfish, though."

Hiro held up a hand and made an O.K. sign.

"Very handsome, your mother's friend," Mariko said, wiping the area around the sink with a rag. "Looks so big and American."

"He's Greek," I said.

Mariko rubbed the counter harder. "Your mother's lucky to have a friend like that. Americans have something, some kind of spark. On the other hand, Japanese men are impossible." She wrung out the rag and hung it over the kitchen faucet to dry. "Short and stupid," she added.

I laughed. "What about Hiro?"

"Hiro," Mariko said, "is the worst." Her voice was toneless, low. She removed her apron, folded it into a trim square, and laid it on the counter. She took a wooden box off the shelf and went into the dining room to count the night's tips.

"You, sit," Hiro said to me, pointing to an empty chair next to Alex. He glanced behind him, reached into his cart, and produced an extra lobster.

"Oh, no, I don't want you to get into trouble," I said, backing away slightly.

"Just don't tell Mariko. Who else counts the lobsters? There are hundreds in that freezer."

"No, really, I'm fine," I protested. After so many summers of smelling steaks and lobsters cooking at the steakhouse, actually eating some seemed more a punishment than a treat.

Alex smiled at me and bowed his head slightly toward Hiro. "He's being nice," he said. "Sit down, we can have a nice conversation. I want to talk to you." Alex tried unsuccessfully to lift some salad with his chopsticks, and finally brought the bowl to his lips.

"About your mother," he added, before scooping lettuce into his mouth.

I watched Hiro's eyebrows lift as he finished oiling the grill. He pulled out a platter of zucchini and onions and began chopping them furiously.

"We'll talk outside," I said.

"What?" Alex said, his voice rising above the clatter.

I cleared my throat. "I'll meet you in the back garden when you're done."

Alex sat forward in his chair, his forearms resting on the table's edge, and stared with delight at Hiro's flashing knives.

Hiro was a little wild making dinner, swinging his decanter of soy sauce so violently that he shot a large slash of it across the front of his apron. When trying to slam a knife back into its holster, he missed, sending it straight into the wooden floor.

His trademark close was to leave a piece of meat or fish on the grill. After bowing and turning to leave, he'd pretend to notice the bit, scoop it deftly on a knife, and send it flying in the air. Tonight, the last piece of lobster soared toward the end of the table, landing squarely on Alex's plate.

WHITE CHRISTMAS LIGHTS twinkled in the trees of the restaurant's backyard. Alex was sitting on a stone bench, his eyes closed, when I came out. I stood across the gravel walk from him, buttoning up my jean jacket as the evening began to cool, and he opened his eyes with a start, his face soft and puffy.

The garden was as satisfyingly scenic as a Hollywood backdrop. There was a round pond with a few carp churning at the bottom, drooping pine trees, and a stone lantern lit with a light bulb. Jagged rocks threw dramatic shadows. Customers often asked to have their picture taken here, smiling for the camera as if on a holiday.

I always enjoyed the garden, which gave me the sensation of being in a foreign place. I liked that feeling, like seeing palm trees out the window when I once visited Florida. It feels off, slightly strange, and even the mundane becomes evocative: the way people cut their hair, the cars they drive, the food they eat.

I wonder what it's like for my mother, each morning when she steps outside her door. Instead of a street lined with low, brown wooden homes, with the sting of salt water heavy in the air, she wakes up to robins singing in trees and a garbage truck rumbling down the street. After thirty years of living here, I wonder if that's what now feels natural and familiar, or if she still feels a jolt from time to time.

"Is Japan really like this?" Alex asked.

"Maybe Tokyo's Disneyland," I replied.

We were silent for a few moments. The wind swirled like water around the nearby trees.

"I think it's important that you and I are friends," Alex said at last.

"Why do we need to be friends?" I asked.

"Why not?"

"Look, Alex, I like you fine. But why do we need to be friends? You're my mother's contractor. That's all."

Through the window, I could see Hiro peering at us from behind the bar. I pinched the collar of my jacket tighter around my neck.

Alex slapped the side of his face. "Who was the chef who cooked for me tonight?" he asked, and checked his palm.

"Hiro."

"He's very talented. All that crazy slicing and dicing."

"No Ginsu knife jokes, please," I said, and Alex laughed.

With each gust of wind, the glittering strings bobbed above us, as if floating on waves.

Alex exhaled loudly, ending with a dry cough into his fist. "So what do you think of your house?" he asked.

"I think it's your business, not mine."

"I suppose it is. But I just wanted to know how you feel, considering how protective you are of your mother."

I laughed unevenly. "I'm not that protective. Sometimes I just have to look out for her."

"It seems to me that looking out for her gives you a kind of purpose," Alex added.

I said nothing.

"She's a strong woman, your mother." Alex spoke quietly while gazing at his hands, which lay open on his lap like water lilies.

"I'm not sure she knows what she wants," I told him. "You seem to be making a lot of the decisions on your own."

"Your mother trusts me."

"You're encouraging her delusions," I said finally. "My mother loves Pavarotti. Maybe *worships* is a better word. And with my father gone, she's that much more vulnerable."

"She seems pretty grounded to me," Alex said gruffly. "She says Pavarotti's coming, and I believe her. There's no reason not to," he said, staring at his hands as if daring them to move.

I sensed the night around us darken and the scent of the pine trees sharpen. The frogs by the pond croaked with an insane fervor. Alex abruptly rose, his back straightening a few moments after his legs, his hand giving my arm an uncertain pat. He walked onto the stone bridge over the circular pond and paused there for a moment, looking at the reflection of the lights in the deep green water. He reached into his pants pocket for a coin, dropped it into the pond, and watched the ripples widen and fade. Then he headed for the parking lot.

BEN CARED ABOUT everything, extending himself in all directions at once, embracing new ideas and ventures with an almost desperate energy.

There were others like him: architecture students who consumed vast quantities of coffee and stayed up all night in order to perfect intricate models that would inevitably end up gathering dust in someone's attic. While they hunched over their books, I thought about all the architects who designed malls and office parks, the anonymous buildings that simply filled space; I thought about the architects who never designed anything because they couldn't find jobs.

I had always loved buildings. Unlike paintings or sculpture, architecture embraced. Whether it be a Romanesque church, a modern library, or a colonial home, the balance of line, proportion, and light aligned my senses in a way that made me understand what the buildings meant—the cozy security of a North American saltbox, the spiritual exultation of a Romanesque cathedral's nave. Even as a child, I had an extremely good sense of proportion—my hopscotch squares were each identical to the next. When I visited my friends, I'd register mentally what was right or wrong with their houses. I never understood why builders put garages in the front, gaping like toothless mouths, or added extensions that followed the original roof line like a tail.

At first, studying architecture was fulfilling. I spent hours drawing the ornate Corinthian columns of the main library, and obsessively researched different types of houses, from Navajo hogans to mansarded French country homes. I knew the difference between cavetto and beak molding, and was fascinated by the buttresses and vaulting of Gothic architecture. But as the coursework grew heavier, I became overwhelmed. There were too many skills to master, too much information to memorize. Physics and calculus classes sapped me of creative energy. I spent few daylight hours outside the studio. My love of architecture, which had inspired me early on, seemed to have dried up and disappeared. I felt as if I were slowly being folded into my studies, like fragile egg whites into a dense batter. And I watched, with irritation yet also amazement, as my classmates transformed themselves.

One boy, formerly nondescript, appeared suddenly with an asymmetrical haircut, wearing perfectly round Philip Johnson glasses. Another boy took to wearing blazing white shirts and neat black pants; he carried an expensive leather backpack and drank coffee from a stainless steel thermos imported from Germany. It was as if they were trying out roles that were not yet naturally theirs. I felt ungainly, having failed to forge an identity for myself. And I began to worry about a future designing layouts for parking garages or, worse, a lifetime of drafting as a bottom feeder at an architectural firm.

I liked Ben. But what I wanted was insurance, a job that would make money and a lifestyle that would avoid the twisty swerves of aspiration. Yearning only created vulnerability. Figuring out that Ben wasn't right for me was easy. All I had to do was listen to the deep sadness of my mother's voice over the phone to know that it was better to be safe.

THE EATING HALL was nearly empty. Late-afternoon light filtered through the trees outside the tall trefoil windows, throwing a lacy, gently undulating shadow on the floor. Ben slipped a quarter into the juke-box, and Tom Jones's muscular voice soon filled the room, asking "What's New, Pussycat?"

"Such an excellent song," he said as he dropped his

backpack onto the table and sat down across from me. He dragged out a series of books from his backpack, followed by an apple and a blackened banana.

"I've decided to call my major 'Modern American Society,'" he said. The school had begun an experimental program that allowed selected students to create their own majors. Ben had eagerly applied. "It'll have a backbone of government and poli-sci courses, and some history, sociology, and English lit thrown in. I'm even going to include some architecture, so maybe we can take a class together."

I sipped my cup of lukewarm coffee. "Sounds interesting," I said.

Ben paused. "What's wrong?"

"To be honest, it seems a little spaced to me."

"Taking architecture?"

I took a deep breath. "'Modern American Society.' I mean, what's the point?"

Ben blinked at me. "Does it have to have a point?"

"Well, we've got less than two years left of college, you know. I'd think you'd want to pursue something more disciplined," I said.

Irritation flickered across Ben's face. We sat in prickly silence for a few seconds.

"I switched majors today," I announced.

"What?"

"I switched out of architecture. I'm getting a degree in accounting."

"Accounting!" Ben gasped. He sounded wounded, as though his lungs had very little air.

"Don't give me a hard time, Ben. I have to do this. I actually have a plan."

Ben laughed weakly. "Sounds very tidy," he said.

"Sometimes I think you and your friends are incredibly naive," I told him.

"Naive?" Ben exclaimed, his voice rising, his face flushed. He shook his head wildly. "Emily, you've got it all wrong."

He bit into his apple, but I could tell he wasn't hungry. He looked at me, mouth closed, his jaw slowly moving, and when he leaned over the table to speak, his breath was sweet with fruit. "You can't protect yourself. And the more you try, the more miserable you'll be."

I wanted to explain to him the intricacies of my family, but I knew Ben would see their problems as only an excuse. What I couldn't tell him was that I had difficulty infusing things with meaning, and that, devoid of meaning, all identities seemed equal to me. I might as well choose one that was practical.

"I'm not afraid," I replied.

We didn't break up until later, but Ben soon stopped staying the night. He never completely moved out of my dorm room. His socks and clean underwear remained in my bottom drawer, his shaving cream and razor on top of my dresser. I wasn't sure whether he had forgotten about

them or if he thought they were too trivial to retrieve. Then we both dissolved into the mass of other students roaming around campus each day, avoiding each other for the remainder of the semester.

Senior year passed quickly for me, a blur of statistics and finance classes. Occasionally, when I sat by a window in the library, I'd see Ben on the arts quad, using his backpack as a pillow. By December, he was with a girl with thick auburn hair.

MY MOTHER SPENT the next morning shopping and returned carrying two big plastic bags emblazoned with the words SYMS: AN EDUCATED CONSUMER IS OUR BEST CUSTOMER.

"Can you believe that at Syms they call the sales clerks 'educators'?" my mother said, dropping the bags to the floor.

"You should buy quality," I told her, looking over the open refrigerator door at my mother's purchases before resuming my search for decent jam.

"I don't need clothes that last," my mother replied. "I'm too old. At a certain age, quality doesn't matter. Do you realize that my new vacuum cleaner is going to outlast me?"

"I hate it when you talk like that."

"Death is part of life," my mother declared brightly, pouring herself a cup of coffee.

After my mother turned fifty-five, she began talking

about death in a strangely pleasant tone of voice. She returned from reunions at the Japan Women's University in Tokyo and told me each time how fewer and fewer people showed up because many had died. She enjoyed the gatherings nonetheless. She would come back happy, calling herself a survivor.

I peered into a jar of jam suspiciously, poking at its contents with a knife. "Why don't you try on some of your new clothes?" I asked.

She did. She paraded around in four different outfits as if in a marching band, pointing each foot in front of her before placing it on the ground. Her chin jutted out at an awkward angle, as if trying to sun itself, and she spun jaunty half turns on her toes. I pictured her twirling a baton.

"They're all by Italian designers," my mother told me. The labels in her clothes did bear Italian names, but I had never heard of any of them—Carlo Andreotti, Nina Giacomo, Donatella Gotti. One of the blouses also had a tiny "Made in Indonesia" tag.

"How would you like to go to a barbecue this Sunday?" she asked, collapsing into a chair.

"Where?" I asked.

"The Kobayashis."

"The Kobayashis! You haven't seen them in years. I thought you didn't like them."

"I don't. But I think it's time to go out. Ever since Pappa

left, I've been locked up in here like a hermit." She paused. "I thought we'd take Alex, too," she added.

"Take Alex? We?"

My mother's pale face quickly darkened to red. "No, not we. Me. I hope you don't mind."

I stopped buttering my toast and shrugged. "It's your life."

"It's a pool party."

The toast I was bringing to my mouth stopped in midair. "You're going to swim?"

My mother smiled. "Why not? Alex says he enjoys swimming. I haven't gone swimming in years."

In fact, she had never learned how to swim, and I had never seen her do anything more than bob nervously in the water while clutching a float. The image of her and Alex wading under the fascinated stares of her Japanese friends made the hairs stand up on the back of my neck.

"Alex says swimming isn't just about swimming," my mother continued. "It's about being in the water, enjoying how it feels. I think that's a nice thing to say."

I took a bite of cold toast. "So are you worried about what people are going to say about you two?" I asked.

My mother looked at me blankly. "I don't know what you mean."

"Oh, come on. You don't think Mrs. Kobayashi's going to be popping out of her skin seeing you with Alex? Even I think it's weird. And I'm your daughter."

"What's so weird about Alex and me as friends? For heaven's sake, *siamo adulti*. It's not like we're doing something bad."

"With all due respect, Mom, he's your contractor, not your friend."

"That's not true. Alex teaches me about the house. I teach him about music, the opera, Luciano. We're opening up new worlds for each other."

CARS LINED BOTH sides of Mulberry Lane in Scarsdale, mostly Japanese-made autos with Ivy League stickers pasted on the rear windows. We pulled up behind a silver Lexus with stickers from Harvard, Yale, and the Massachusetts Institute of Technology.

"Do you know what MIT really stands for?" I asked from the backseat.

Only Alex seemed interested. "What?" he said.

"Made In Taiwan."

Alex laughed. The Kobayashis lived in a stone house with a gravel horseshoe driveway and a tiled pool in the back. There was a separate brick garage for Mr. Kobayashi's cars.

"They like to show their money," my mother told Alex. He held his forearm out like a rail so she could grasp it while getting out of the car. He nodded and straightened his collar with his free hand.

They walked ahead of me, Alex in khakis and a dark

blue blazer and my mother dressed like an Italian movie star—large black sunglasses, a simple black shirt with matching black stretch pants. Despite my protests, she wore a flowered chiffon scarf over her head and tied at the chin, à la Sophia Loren.

Alex looked as if he was moving in slow motion, his wide stride timed to my mother's shorter gait.

"Hanako-san. Over here." Mrs. Kobayashi called to us from a slate path leading around the side of her house. She was dressed in a denim dirndl skirt and white blouse, an Hermès scarf draped over her shoulders and tied in front. She waved using her entire arm, as if we might miss her and move on to another house. From the street, I could hear people talking in the backyard, then a splash in the pool. My mother closed her mouth and smiled as she walked up the slate steps.

BEFORE MRS. KOBAYASHI could bow in greeting, my mother leaned awkwardly toward her face to kiss her on both carefully powdered cheeks. Mrs. Kobayashi blushed and laughed nervously, covering her mouth with her hand.

"My, Hanako, you've become so Continental," she said.

"I'm afraid I can't fight it," my mother replied.

"And Emily, how are you?" Mrs. Kobayashi asked. "Takeshi is returning from college today. You remember Takeshi, don't you?"

I nodded at Mrs. Kobayashi unenthusiastically. When I was about twelve, I had played with Takeshi, a soft, unco-ordinated boy with braces, spiky hair, and thick glasses that made his eyes look huge. Charlotte and I had bossed him around, calling him "Takenoko," Japanese for Bamboo Shoot.

"And, and this must be?" Mrs. Kobayashi looked past me at Alex.

"Signore Alex Pappadopolous," my mother said.

"Oh, buon giorno, signore," Mrs. Kobayashi said proudly. My mother, Alex, and I gathered in a small group facing her.

"I'm American," Alex said. "I speak English."

Mrs. Kobayashi, her forehead tight with confusion, smiled.

"Of course. How silly of me. Welcome, welcome to our home. Let's join the party," she said, leading us along the slate walk that led around to the back of the house.

She offered Alex a crystal bowl of olives from a picnic table, and he pricked one with a toothpick.

"We noticed your new door when we drove by a few days ago," Mrs. Kobayashi said to my mother, watching Alex.

"I'm fixing the house," my mother said. She stood with her hands clasped behind her back, sunglasses now perched atop her head. I had never seen her stand that way before. "Alex is helping me."

"Oh, really!" Mrs. Kobayashi exclaimed. "We've done some work on our house, too."

Mrs. Kobayashi put the bowl of olives down on the table and passed around a tray of crackers and cheese. "Do you do a lot of work in Westchester?" she asked, as Alex selected a cube of cheddar with his free hand.

He shook his head. "Not too much. I work mainly in Putnam County. I live in Brewster."

"Oh. A lovely area."

Mrs. Kobayashi's smile quivered, and she turned to me. "And what are you doing now? You must have graduated recently, no? Any marriage proposals?"

I felt myself break into a difficult smile, my upper lip disappearing over my gums. "I'm waiting for the right man."

"And how can it not happen?" Alex interrupted. "She's a catch."

I looked at him in surprise. He smiled, still holding the toothpick with its olive impaled on the end, the cube of cheese in his other hand.

Mrs. Kobayashi clapped her hands together once, a diamond winking in the sun. "She is!"

I scanned her bosky backyard, filled with people, and recognized faces from years ago, from parties in our own backyard when my parents were active in Westchester's Japanese community: Mrs. Honda, whose husband worked for Toyota; the Arakis; the Takitanis; the Ozakis. Many were looking our way. At first, I assumed they were curious about Alex, but then I realized that most hadn't seen me in years. They probably remembered me as a polite little girl, standing by my mother's side, as I was doing now. My parents had arrived in America before all these friends, and for a time our family had been the centerpiece of Westchester's tight-knit Japanese community. The tiny world they created was like Japan all over again.

Mr. Kobayashi was grilling steaks and burgers at a large brick barbecue pit, and Mrs. Kobayashi waved when he looked up. His face brightened and she motioned for him to join us. He came over, still wearing an apron.

"Well, it's been a long time," he said, patting my mother's back. "So good to see you."

Alex thrust out his right hand. "Hanako's told me a lot about you," he said.

"Alex is a builder," Mrs. Kobayashi told her husband, who was shaking Alex's hand vigorously.

"Well, carpenter really," Alex said, flushing slightly. "Nothing as big as a builder."

"A man who works with his hands," Mr. Kobayashi said kindly.

"That's right." Alex nodded. "That's right."

"I've always admired men who can do things with their hands. My hands, on the other hand, are soft and weak," Mr. Kobayashi said, holding them out, as if for inspection, his nails as pearly as the inside of a shell.

MR. KOBAYASHI EXCUSED himself to tend his grill while Mrs. Kobayashi announced she wanted to show my mother her new kitchen.

"Nice people," Alex said, before finally inserting the olive in his mouth and pulling it off the toothpick. We watched Mrs. Kobayashi, talking animatedly, lead my silent mother back toward the house.

"I haven't seen them since Pappa left," I said.

"Why not?" he asked.

"My mother was sort of embarrassed, or ashamed, something like that."

"You're kidding. Your mother carries herself with such confidence."

"She does?"

"Very much so."

"She worried a lot about what the Japanese thought after the divorce. Since then she's preferred being with Western friends, partly because of her European interests, but I think mainly because they don't know her past. She always says she wished Pappa had died, and how much easier it would be to tell people she was a widow."

"Oh, she has no idea," Alex said, chewing on the toothpick. "My wife died. Breast cancer. It was a terrible thing."

"I'm sorry, Alex," I said, suddenly aware of him for the first time as a person beyond his role as a contractor.

He removed the toothpick, slipped the cheese square he had been holding into his mouth, and ate it silently. "It's good your mother feels comfortable here again, with her old friends," he said, twirling the toothpick in his fingers. "Old friends can't be replaced."

A boy in red swimming briefs ran past and jumped into the pool, spraying us with water. Alex turned his face away and laughed, opening his mouth wide, his teeth square and even.

"EMILY! ALEX! WOULD you like to come inside and have a look at our house?" Mrs. Kobayashi called out from an open kitchen window.

Alex looked at me. "Shall we?" he asked, sticking out his arm, elbow first, in my direction. After a slight hesitation, I hooked my fingers on his arm, and we walked up the back steps.

Mrs. Kobayashi apologized for the inadequacy of her house, her poor decorating skills, and dirty windows when, in fact, the house was huge, the rooms tastefully, if showily, appointed, and the windows as clear as air.

"The house from the outside is postmodernist," Mrs. Kobayashi said, her tone confidential, as if disclosing a family secret.

"What does that mean, postmodernist?" asked Alex, as we stood in the kitchen.

Mrs. Kobayashi looked at him blankly for an instant. "Historical details integrated with contemporary design," she said and gave us a smile.

She laughed lightly, her arms floating as she gestured to the loveliness around her: Lustrous wooden floors, stained the color of chestnuts, met seamlessly with the creamy walls; tiny recessed lights dotted the ceiling. "You can imagine the challenges that presented on the inside. My architect and interior decorator both had different ideas. And matching what they thought with what the contractor could do! Such trouble!"

"Alex has been able to do everything so far," my mother said. "Of course, my needs are far simpler than yours," she added. She stood back to take in a small Baccarat chandelier glittering mightily overhead.

She and Alex exchanged a brief glance. I thought they might both be embarrassed, my mother by Mrs. Kobayashi's obvious talent for decorating, and Alex by the quality of the work that had been done. It was as if the limits of both their worlds had been rudely delineated. But I detected nothing more than simple acknowledgment between them, my mother smiling and Alex nodding in response.

MAYBE IT'S A blessing that children don't see their parents courting. It's rarely as pure as children would like to think. Relationships can burst into existence for flimsy reasons—when a furtive glance leads to physical attraction or when friendships combust into lust. Some people look to each other to save themselves from overpowering loneliness. Thinking of my parents today, such different individuals, I can't fathom why they got together.

"YOUR SKYLIGHTS ARE wonderful," my mother told Mrs. Kobayashi as we walked down the steps into the backyard. Mrs. Kobayashi nodded, adjusting the scarf on her small, sloped shoulders.

"They add so much warmth to the kitchen," she said, and looped her arm in my mother's.

My mother turned to Alex. "Should we have put skylights in?" she asked.

"We still can if you'd like," Alex replied, a thin sheen of perspiration coating his forehead. He shifted into the shade of a maple tree.

Overhearing the conversation as he walked up behind them, Mr. Kobayashi glanced toward Alex and smiled. "Women," he said.

Alex laughed uneasily and speared two pieces of cheese with a fresh toothpick. He laid one piece neatly on a cracker and offered it to me off his dry, coarse hand.

As I watched my mother at the party, I could see an eagerness in her face as she tried to read how she was being judged even as each guest tried to disguise a deep curiosity about her. While she always seemed above humiliation, infused with authority, she could be like me—craving companionship or approval, vulnerable to rejection.

She had put her sunglasses on again, and I imagined her

envisioning how exotic she must appear compared to the conservative, corporate types here at the party. ("And to arrive with a mysterious, handsome man—they must all be shocked!" I imagined her thinking.) After so many years of absence from this group, I knew she sought their admiration and approval. Yet she also seemed to want to show she was no longer really one of them.

Her Japanese friends greeted her with careful, guarded courtesy, and I watched them whisper as soon as my mother and Alex moved on. I wanted to see some reaction that my mother could relish, but there was none.

Still, Alex was a natural, making loud pronouncements about the necessity to cook hamburgers until they were well-done, chatting pleasantly about the weather, laughing about the swimming trunks he had brought.

I could see she enjoyed the companionship. And as I stood watching them, sipping a cold drink by myself, I felt something like envy.

"Oh, here comes Takeshi," Mrs. Kobayashi said, turning to me. "Takeshi!" she called out, gesturing with her hand. "He's really our guest of honor today. Come here, stand beside me." She beamed. "I am proud to introduce Takeshi, graduate-student-to-be at the California Institute of Technology. Is that the correct full name?"

Takeshi came to his mother's side and smiled. He stood over six feet tall, but his large, soft face was still the same as when he was a child, lips only a shade darker than his pallid skin, his nose broad at the base and speckled with perspiration. A crewcut tamed his stiff hair. The only thing that was different was his clothing; instead of the white shirt and shorts, he wore loose blue jeans cinched at the waist with a black belt and a T-shirt with a large question mark on the front. The thick glasses were gone—replaced, I assumed, by contact lenses.

"You and your sister used to pick on me," he said, breaking into a smile. His teeth were still bad.

I laughed dryly, trying to avoid his gaze.

"Just don't call me Takenoko anymore. That really does wonders for a boy's ego."

Mrs. Kobayashi nudged her son's elbow. "Takeshi, say hello to Mrs. Shimoda. You remember her, don't you? And of course, this is her friend, Alex."

"Hi." Takeshi extended a tanned hand to Alex, who shook it firmly. "Good to see you again, Mrs. Shimoda," he said, turning to my mother. "You're looking well."

My mother, pleased, reached to touch her hair. Feeling her scarf, she removed it, evidently having forgotten she'd left it on for so long.

"Congratulations on Caltech. What will you be studying?" she asked.

Takeshi grinned. "Biochemistry. I'm a bit of a nerd, unlike your daughter."

I felt myself flush, and my ears began to tingle.

"So, what are you up to these days, Emily?" he asked. I

checked his face for some sign of sarcasm, but found only goodwill.

"I just got out of school. I'm waiting tables for now," I replied.

"I thought you'd be doing something creative. You used to draw pictures of me. They were really good. You got everything down, my glasses, my braces—"

"Your short shorts," I added.

Takeshi laughed.

"Our family does have artistic inclinations," my mother said loudly.

"Oh, there are the Hondas. You must meet the Hondas," Mrs. Kobayashi told Alex, pointing to a couple in their late forties, both dressed in matching white sweaters.

"I'm looking forward to meeting all of Hanako's friends," Alex replied.

"They're renovating their garage. They want to convert it into a billiards room."

Alex blinked. "Is that right?" he asked.

"I'm sure if you work for Hanako, they'll want to hire you right away." She turned to Takeshi. "Why don't you entertain Emily for a while? She tells us she's unattached!"

I watched Mrs. Kobayashi weave her way through her garden of guests, leading my mother and an uncertain Alex by the arm, his blazer now hanging neatly over his shoulder.

• • •

I THOUGHT OF the last time I saw Ben. We were standing on the football field, a few minutes after our graduating class had thrown caps in the air with forced (at least for me) cheer. Ben was in complete disarray, his cheeks and nose ruddy from champagne, his gown unzipped to reveal a dingy undershirt, gym shorts, and pale, hairy legs.

"Well, good-bye," I said.

He laughed. "That's cold, Emily. Even for you."

I wasn't purposefully trying to be distant. I just didn't know what else to say.

"I'm going to study in Beijing in the fall," he said. "But first I'm going to Vietnam! I'm really excited."

"That's great, Ben."

We stood in silence. Although there was a storm of activity around us, the space between Ben and me was strangely quiet. The broad blue sky seemed to infuse the football field with its clarity. I felt as if I could count all the golden hairs on Ben's head, each strand radiantly defined by the sun.

We remained motionless until he scratched one of several mosquito bites on his legs.

"So what are you going to do?" he asked.

I had a couple of practiced answers ready. But when I looked at Ben, I couldn't form the words in my throat.

"I'm going home," I replied.

Ben started to reach for my arm but stopped when his

fingers touched me. I felt a flutter, as if a butterfly had brushed against my skin.

"Good-bye," he said.

"YOU SEEM EXCITED about Caltech," I said to Takeshi, who was staring at the pool.

He shrugged. "Well, yeah. I've always been good at math and science, ever since I was a kid. I wish I could do something to shock everyone, though, like become a toll-booth collector. Wow, would that freak my parents out."

"I don't think that would make your mother too happy."

"What did you study in school?"

"Architecture. Well, at least until my junior year. Then, for a lot of reasons, I switched majors."

"To what?"

"Accounting."

We watched Mrs. Kobayashi emerge from the house carrying half a gigantic watermelon, scraped clean, and filled with red, green, and orange melon balls. She teetered uncertainly at the top step, adjusted the watermelon in her hands, and started her descent.

"Because of your parents?" Takeshi asked.

"Actually, it was because of my mother that I got interested in architecture—Romanesque architecture really—but my parents split up, and I got a little nervous about my future, so I caved in and switched."

"That's too bad. You seem more the artistic type than a

bean counter." Takeshi bent over to firmly adjust a Velcro strap on an ugly black sandal. "You always seemed so sure about yourself back then. I was so impressed."

"Thanks, though it's been a long time since I've drawn anything."

We sat in silence for a while, watching the people around us talk and eat, and for the first time that afternoon, I began to relax.

ALEX EMERGED FROM one of the green-curtained cabanas wearing a large white T-shirt and knee-length electric-orange trunks with a green stripe around each thigh. Both the trunks and the shirt looked brand-new. He stood at one end of the pool and dipped his foot into the iridescent blue water.

"It's awfully cold," he called out to me.

"Where's my mother?" I asked.

"Changing," he replied. The sun had drifted lower in the late-afternoon sky, and most of the guests were gone. Alex jumped up and down beside the pool.

"You know, they say the way people enter pools says a lot about the way they make love," Takeshi said conspiratorially. He had come from the kitchen, carrying two iced teas. Sweat glimmered through his black hair.

A faint fragrance of soap reached me as he sat on the wood deck next to my chair, wrapping his arms around his knees.

"People who are shy and cautious in bed take forever to get in the water," Takeshi said. "Bolder types jump right in."

Alex cupped his hands and directed his voice in the direction of the cabanas. "Hanako!" he called out.

"Yes, yes," my mother replied, irritation tinging her muffled voice. The curtain of her cabana fluttered. A few moments later, she emerged.

My mother had always been a modest woman. When she took us to public pools as kids, she'd hardly ever change out of her clothes, only donning a suit on the hottest days. I hadn't seen her in a swimsuit for over fifteen years. Still, I immediately recognized the one she had on. It was flowered diagonally across the front, a pleated skirt covering the tops of her thighs. Her body filled the suit to near-bursting, the elastic fabric compressing folds of flesh at her breasts and stomach. She looked very white in the sunlight, except for several small bruises on her legs.

"You look lovely, Hanako," Alex called out as my mother passed quickly by. She walked toward the shallow end, stone-faced, and seated herself at the pool's edge with her feet in the water. After studying the water's surface, she glanced up at me, her face tight with strain.

"She's that way because she can't swim well," I told Takeshi, trying to hide my embarrassment. Alex suddenly pulled the T-shirt up over his head to reveal a surprisingly muscular chest, filled with fluffy white hair. He was deeply tanned from the elbows to his hands, and from his neck to the tips of his ears. But the rest of his body was a porcelain white, as if belonging to another person. He swung his arms in the air, much as my father did before swimming, and I wondered if that was something all men of a certain age did around pools.

"Proper warm-up is important," Alex said to no one in particular, his words barely audible under his heavy breathing. "You don't want to get cramps."

He performed a series of deep knee bends, eyes straight ahead, focused on the back door of the Kobayashi house. My mother watched him warily.

Mr. Takitani swam toward the shallow end, eyeglasses still perched on his nose, his silver hair combed smoothly over his scalp. He stared at Alex and then at my mother before eventually bumping into the wall.

"Is that you, Hanako-san?" Mr. Takitani stood up and removed his glasses. He shook water from the lenses before returning them to his nose.

"Takitani-san, so good to see you," my mother called out, bowing her head slightly.

Mr. Takitani glanced at Alex again before speaking.

"How are you?" he asked.

"Very fine, thank you."

"You're looking well. Very sporty."

"Thank you," she said.

He looked cautiously at Alex, who offered a quick wave

before embarking on a series of jumping jacks. "I'm Alex," he called out, "a friend of Hanako's."

My mother lowered her eyes and gazed at the water, the ends of her mouth turned up slightly in a smile.

"I see," Mr. Takitani said. "A pleasure to meet you."

"Likewise."

Mr. Ozaki, floating on his back, bobbed upright as Alex jogged lightly in a small circle, his arms jiggling at his sides.

"Now, quick, tell me how you think Alex will get in the pool," Takeshi said excitedly. "Quick, quick."

"I say he's going to dive in, all at once, and get the cold over with," I said.

Takeshi shook his head, a thin gold chain glimmering at his neck. "No, he doesn't look that aggressive. He's got a few inhibitions. No, I think he'll sit at the side of the pool, and kind of lower himself in."

A breeze rippled the water, and Alex stopped, facing the pool, his toes kneading the soft ground. Then he broke into a run, arms pumping at his sides, until he reached the tiled edge. Leaping in the air, he squeezed his body into a tight ball, suspended for a moment like a planet, before cracking the water's surface with an enormous splash.

SEVEN

My mother lit a candle and placed it on the kitchen table, the quivering light warming her otherwise pale face. We sat in silence, the slow evening uninterrupted by any other noise in the house, the air so still and quiet that I thought I might hear the melting wax drip.

"Fire is an amazing, beautiful thing," she said, leaning back in her chair, the details of her features receding into the darkness.

"Yeah, well so is electricity," I replied.

Our power had been turned off sometime the night before. The refrigerator abruptly stopped, leaving its contents to wilt. When I touched the bottles and containers inside that morning, they were all coated with condensation and retained only a faint chill.

"Sort of romantic, isn't it?" my mother remarked, crossing her arms over her chest. "Candlelight. Silence. Night. It's inspiring."

She sang a high tune, in a minor key. I knew the melody well: "Okesa," a folk song about the first people to arrive on Sado Island. In Japan, men and women danced to the music, wearing taut kimonos, straw hats tipped to cover their faces. My mother barely moved her mouth as she sang; the music was as natural to her as breathing. "Sado eh to kusa ki mo nabi-ku yo," she sang, until the point at which others are cued to chime, "Ah-ryo, ah-ryo, ah-ryo-san." But, in our kitchen, there was only silence.

"I miss Sado," my mother said.

"Why?" I asked. "It's full of old people, with nothing to do but eat fish and drink beer."

My mother only sang Japanese songs when she felt sad and only talked about the island when unhappy with her life here. Sado was actually a wonderful place. Snow remained on the mountaintops until mid-June and ravens hovered in the pine trees over garden ponds, cawing at the carp. The air was clear and smelled of the sea.

"When I was in primary school, a servant from my house would deliver my box lunch to school every day at noon," she said, smiling. "I don't remember this exactly, but my friends have told me this is the way it was. I guess that's why the food always tasted so fresh."

"When *was* the last time you paid the electricity bill?" I

asked. "And aren't you having the singing group over tomorrow?"

"This isn't such a big problem, you know. For the time being, try and enjoy the evening." We fell silent, both staring at the candle's silent flame.

I ONLY KNEW my father within the context of family rituals—a quiet presence behind a morning newspaper as my mother scrambled eggs, an impatient man behind the wheel of his Chevrolet taking us shopping for new rakes. My mother was eternally accessible, her constant, solitary vigil in the kitchen exposing her to all of us. But the whirl of the family provided a veil through which my father's true self was shaded. After he left, I felt as though he had been enclosed in an unconnected room in our house, living a separate, parallel life all along.

If I moved with my father to France, we would both be freed from all that we were before. My mother's chaotic house, Ben's disapproval, the steakhouse would all disappear. I would wear perfume and smoke clove cigarettes. People would judge me on my mysterious appearance rather than any actual knowledge, and I imagined comfort in that kind of superficiality. My parents must have felt that way when they moved to America: my mother leaving behind a privileged childhood drained of its wealth by the war, my father a trying past that would have drained others of hope. Moving to a new place allowed them to reinvent themselves.

It occurred to me that my brother, Pierre, had wanted to be liberated as well when he left us for Milan. I had always thought him a happy boy, although he was difficult to read. His large forehead, sharp cheekbones, heavy eyebrows, and strong chin lacked the soft elasticity needed for emotional expression and, as a result, his face revealed little. But I always sensed that he was impatient with us. I pictured him at an outdoor café in Milan, eating gelatos with his painter friends, smiling faintly.

Then I imagined my father in his pajamas, sitting at the head of a long banquet table in our château. I'd be seated at the other end, two large candelabras between us. Did it seem strange to him to have six empty bedrooms and a fireplace big enough to roast a deer on a spit? I wanted to believe that the majestic past of the home's previous occupants would more than compensate for the fact that none of what Pappa and I had was really ours.

MY MOTHER LIT a second candle for me and got up, holding hers on a saucer as she headed upstairs. I watched as she paused momentarily in front of Charlotte's clean, orderly room before going into her own. When she was gone, I noticed a postcard for me on the kitchen table. The card, from Happy Life Serviced Apartments in Tokyo, showed a tall, tiled building on a busy city street and two views of a typical room's interior: a single bed, writing desk, desk lamp, dresser, love seat, tiny refrigerator, microwave, and two-burner stove. "My new home!" my father's neat handwriting read on the other side. "The entire bathroom—bathtub, sink, and floor—was molded from a single piece of plastic. Very near many subway stations. Please come visit. Love, Father."

As I carried the postcard and the candle upstairs, I noticed a glow through the half-open door of my mother's bedroom. She was kneeling on the floor by the side of her bed, going through mail piled up near her pillow. She methodically opened envelopes and unfolded bills, and sorted them into separate stacks. Her candle had burned down to an inch of white wax, but she continued at her slow pace, as if she had all night to devote to the task.

After changing into a nightgown, I got into bed and looked at the card again. I pictured my father lying beneath his single bed's clean white sheets, the soft ticking of the apartment's alarm clock lulling him to sleep, his beloved subway cars rumbling somewhere deep beneath the floor of his new home.

For my mother, a home was a way of creating her own world within a world of uncertainty. My father's home, I realized, would never be the physical environment around him, but a feeling he carried with him, no matter where he was.

Perhaps if my home was with my mother, in her

builder's house on Hunting Ridge Hollow, or with my father in a French château, my own life couldn't really begin. That's what Ben probably meant about being afraid to find my own place in the world, I thought.

THE NEXT MORNING I came downstairs for breakfast. My mother stood distracted and listless by the kitchen sink, her fingers toying with a button on her blouse.

"Are you all right?" I asked.

She hesitated. "Did I ever tell you about when my mother died?" she asked, looking out the window.

I shook my head.

"She was in the hospital with cancer, and was allowed only one visitor to remain with her until late. One night, we all sensed it would be her last. And she still had to pick only one person."

My mother brushed a strand of hair from her face and laughed quietly. "She chose my sister-in-law. She was the one who had been there on the island, seeing her through her illness. I suppose it was natural that she would pick her over me."

My mother didn't act particularly disturbed by the memory, although I couldn't imagine her opting for someone who wasn't her own child.

"So my sister-in-law stayed that night," my mother continued, putting on a pair of rubber gloves. "And she was the one with my mother when she died."

I handed her a stack of cups and saucers, which she placed gently in the sink. We stood silently by each other, not moving.

"The Sado house is gone," she told me.

"What do you mean it's gone?"

"My brother sold it to a developer. He told me in a letter I read last night. He couldn't keep it up."

The house was the biggest on the island and seemed as permanently fixed in our lives as a river or mountain. Even I could feel the tug of the house, knowing that part of my history was preserved, safe, under a roof in Japan. I wished something uncontrollable had happened to it. Being blasted by a tidal wave or collapsed by an earthquake were appropriately drastic scenarios for such a grand old home. To simply fall victim to a bulldozer and a backhoe seemed trivial, humiliating.

The singers were coming soon, and although it was only late morning, the day already felt long and drawn out, as if it should be dark.

My mother turned the water on and began rinsing the cups. "The buyer wants to tear the house down and put up a building," she said. "My brother tried to hold out for someone who wants to live in the place, but no one did. It's just too big."

She put a soapy hand to her chest. *"Mi fa male qui,"* she said.

"What does that mean?" I asked.

"It hurts here," she replied.

We stood there, water from the faucet running into the sink, until we heard voices, talking and laughing, on our front steps.

BERNARD AND INGE arrived first, both dressed in crisp white linen shirts, creased blue jeans, and huarache sandals. Bernard pressed a satchel to his side as he leapt up our front stairs.

"Good to see you, Hanako," he said, pulling out a hand-kerchief from his back pocket and dabbing at his face before kissing my mother.

"Thank you for coming," my mother replied, smiling, her face white and matte, like unbaked bread.

"Very warm today, isn't it?"

"Oh, I'm never one to get very hot," my mother replied, showing the couple into the living room. "The renovation is going so well," Inge said, sitting on the sofa. She rubbed her bare feet on the floor. "Lovely," she exclaimed.

Gisela and Lynne came a few minutes later, talking loudly as they walked up our driveway, their laughing oddly musical, as if following a score. The warm sweet scent of gardenias permeated the air as soon as Gisela came in the house.

"Hot day!" Gisela exclaimed, collapsing into a damp heap on a chair.

"Terrible," my mother said, pouring tepid, sun-steeped

tea into glasses, wiping drips off the coffee table with a white napkin.

"I absolutely cannot sing under these conditions," Bernard said, shaking his head as he opened his satchel and riffled through his music. "Hanako, would it be possible to have some air-conditioning?"

"We're having some problems with our electricity," I said, looking at my mother.

She smiled slightly, and smoothed her hair with her hand. "Unfortunately, we can't use the air conditioner. But that shouldn't prevent us from singing, should it?"

Gisela snorted. "I once sang at an outdoor concert in Baltimore in August, the hottest day of the year. The conditions were deplorable. Humidity, pollution, little bugs flying into my mouth, everything! But I sang, Bernie. It doesn't matter where you are. You have to want to sing."

Still seated, Gisela began singing. Her voice was as languorous as her body, and the scented air filled with her soulful notes. My mother walked toward where I stood in the corner of the room.

"'Summertime,'" she whispered. "From *Porgy and Bess*."

"I know, I know. George Gershwin," I replied.

My mother turned her head to me in surprise.

Gisela finished with a dramatic flourish, snapping her hands into fists as if trying to grasp the air. We applauded, my mother the most loudly. "Hanako, dear, do you have any ice for this?" Gisela asked, holding up her tea.

"I'm terribly sorry, Gisela, but the refrigerator also can't be used," my mother said.

"Of course, of course. No problem."

There was an uneasy silence.

"Speaking of hot air, have you heard about Pavarotti?" Gisela said, her face still pink from singing. "Carousing around with that girl instead of his wife."

"What girl?" Inge asked.

"Some pretty young thing. Young enough to be his daughter," Gisela sniffed.

"It's deterioration," my mother said, her hands clasped together primly on her lap. "If your body cells are intact, this kind of thing doesn't happen."

"What do you mean?" Gisela asked.

"To have an affair with some person and dumping whatever you've built up for the past thirty or forty years —that's a sign of deterioration. I can see that in Pavarotti. He can see his future and that is very scary."

"He is almost sixty," Lynne added.

My mother nodded sharply. "Look at Domingo. He's doing well, despite his age. Either he didn't have this, how shall I call it, offshoot, or he had it and cut it off."

"Ouch," Bernard said.

"It's like the offshoot of a plant," my mother continued, one arm slithering into the air. "It saps you of energy. Domingo sticks with the same old woman and stays healthy. Pavarotti doesn't, and is sapped."

I put a plate of cookies down on the table and tried to meet my mother's gaze, which remained fixed on the floor. The singers paused again, the warm air in the room seemingly stifling their usual energy. I watched a drop of sweat slip down Gisela's normally cool, dry face.

"Your house is looking wonderful, Hanako," Inge said. "It will be terrific when it's finished."

Bernard inserted a cookie into his mouth as he pulled out a folder from his satchel marked "Puccini." He chuckled as he held out a song. "Well, this is relatively easy. I could always sing this—" he began.

"I want to sing," my mother announced.

Bernard reached into his bag. "Wait a minute, wait a minute, I've got the tape player in here," he said, his mouth full of cookie.

"No tape," my mother said.

She strode to the fireplace and stood in front of the mantelpiece, her hands tightened into determined fists. She wavered, and unclasped her hands for balance.

"Ahhh, Sado eh," she began. She drew out the notes for as long as she could, slipping slowly through lilting half notes sweet and plaintive. Her eyes were big and unblinking. I remembered dancing the Okesa during summer evenings, trying my best to mimic the adults, the air cool and salty, my feet swimming in borrowed sandals. My father never danced, standing off to the side, smoking, the lit end of his cigar blinking on and off like a firefly. But my mother danced, her face luminescent as the moon, her arms and hands sweeping through the air.

"Sado eh to kusa ki mo nabi-ku yo," my mother sang.

And then I sang back: "Ah-ryo, ah-ryo, ah-ryo-san." My mother glanced at me calmly, without surprise, as if she had been expecting me to join her. I listened to her carefully, singing the chorus each time she reached the refrain, until she finally finished the "Okesa."

The room was silent. Gisela was staring at my mother, her chin balanced on a finger, while Bernard and Inge exchanged glances. My mother remained in front of the fireplace for a few moments, looking out the window, before speaking.

"I'm terribly sorry for all the discomfort," she said. "Perhaps it would be best if we stopped here for today."

MY MOTHER AND I were in the kitchen when the garage door opened. I listened to the stairs creak, then Alex turned the corner, dressed in white painter's pants and a cantaloupe-colored T-shirt, his hair freshly combed. He had a clear, confident air, as if he had just emerged from a shower to begin his day. I felt a sense of relief when I saw him.

My mother, standing on top of a step stool, returning a tin of biscotti to a high shelf, shook her head. "Oh, Alex," she said, pressing her closed eyelids with a thumb and forefinger. "We don't have power today. So I'm afraid we won't be able to work on the bathroom. Maybe you can come back some other time. Is that possible? I'll call you when we have this problem solved."

He looked at both of us from the hallway.

"Are you O.K.?" he asked.

My mother nodded. "Please just come back some other time," she said, suddenly unsteady on her feet. She swayed for a second, arms flailing as she groped the air for balance, and then she stepped off the stool and slowly crumpled to the floor, still clutching the biscotti tin. Her head made a surprisingly soft thud when it hit the floor.

I watched this happen from the kitchen table as if it was a home movie, demanding from its audience only muted amazement. Even leaning over my mother, her face white and slack, her mouth slightly open, I still couldn't believe that I was there, present.

"Mom?" I asked, my voice sounding in my head as if my ears were blocked.

Alex shuffled quickly into the kitchen, his workboots heavy against the tile, dropped to his knees, and carefully picked up my mother's head as if retrieving a fallen melon. I stood by dumbly.

"Get on the phone and call someone," Alex instructed. His voice turned gentle. "Hanako? Hanako? Hello?"

My mother's eyelids fluttered open to reveal the whites of her eyes. She raised her left hand and touched my knee.

"I'm fine. Don't call anyone. I just lost my balance."

She managed to prop herself up on her elbows.

Alex glared at me, his right eyebrow arched dramatically. "Call a doctor, Emily," he demanded.

My mother looked at me pleadingly. She hated doctors. When I was a child, she suffered alone through bouts of bronchitis, poison ivy, and a mild case of what we later concluded had been pneumonia. She simply climbed into bed and stayed buried under the covers until she recovered.

"I have very low blood pressure," she told Alex. "I have to be careful about getting too tired. I need to keep stimulants in my body." She tilted herself to her right side, rolled onto her knees, and struggled to her feet, her back toward Alex.

"I'm going upstairs to lie down a minute," she said hoarsely.

Alex stood up, brushing invisible particles from his knees, scenting the room with turpentine. He watched my mother straighten her sweatshirt and leave the kitchen.

"Frankly, I'm all for doctors," he said.

"My mother's fine. She has this low blood pressure thing every now and again. It's nothing to worry about."

"How old is your mother?"

"Fifty-eight this past April."

"And when she falls down in front of you, you don't get worried."

I knew how strong my mother could be. A day in bed, and she would be all right. "What good does it do to worry?" I asked.

"You're her child. That's your job."

I shot Alex a look. "How old are you?"

He appeared startled. "Sixty-five. No, sixty-six." He ran his hand through his hair. "I just turned sixty-six. In January."

"What sort of kids do you have? They don't worry about you doing this kind of work?"

Alex paused for a moment, then he headed to the living room and stood at the bottom of the stairs. "I'll check on you in a while, O.K., Hanako?" he said loudly. His baritone voice resounded in the hallway.

My mother didn't answer. I sat alone in the kitchen, listening to Alex go down through the garage to his truck and start the engine.

MY MOTHER'S BEDROOM was exactly as it was when my father was living at home; there was a wooden dresser with a mirror cracked in one corner, two bedside tables, a double bed, and a desk that rocked when you wrote on it. The walls, curtains, and bedspread were off-white, really of no color at all. Pappa's books were still piled in teetering stacks on the floor, and his silk ties hung in the closet.

When I peeked in, my mother was deep beneath a tangle of sheets, only the top of her head visible from where I stood.

"Feeling better?" I asked, nearing the mound of covers. There was slight movement, and I heard deep, even breathing. She moaned a little before pulling the sheets down to reveal her pale face.

"You gave me a scare down there," I told her, sitting beside her on the bed.

"Actually, the experience was quite strange," my mother said. "I see the biscotti, and suddenly I don't see them anymore. Next thing is Alex's face in front of me."

"He was worried."

"Oh, please. How embarrassing. There is no need." She paused, smiling slightly. "Although I must admit it is rather nice of Alex to be concerned," she added.

"Can I get you anything?" I asked.

"If it's not too much trouble, could you go out and buy me some broccoli rabe? I feel like I need some green vegetables, iron. They sell it at the Chinese restaurant."

"Sure. I'll go out and get some."

"Thank you."

Despite the stifling heat in her room, my mother buried herself again under the sheet, as if preparing to hibernate for the winter. By the time I had gotten up and reached the door, she was already snoring softly.

• • •

As I TURNED onto the main street in town, I spotted Alex's green truck pausing at a stoplight, several cars in front of me. Instead of making a left to go to the restaurant, I decided to follow him. He waved to a gardener mowing a lawn, who froze for a moment, as if unable to make out Alex's face through his perspiration, before jumping to attention.

"My man!" he yelled.

I slowed to a crawl on each straightaway, speeding up only after Alex's truck had disappeared around a bend ahead. He made his way through Pleasant Springs' leafy neighborhoods to the Saw Mill River Parkway. He wove through light traffic, light blue smoke shooting out his truck's exhaust pipe, braking politely for a driver who swerved suddenly in front of him. He continued to head north, passing the exits for Mount Kisco and Bedford Hills, driving with one arm out the window, his hand lightly tapping the car door. I hardly ever traveled this far north; my life as a child ended at the Bedford Hills' McDonald's and the nearby shopping mall. Alex took the exit ramp toward Brewster and his truck zoomed along with increasing confidence, working the twisting streets of familiar territory.

We continued like this for a while, with a Buick and a van evenly spaced between us, passing by expanses of open land. I started to enjoy not knowing where it would end, and loosened my hands on the steering wheel, nearly missing Alex when he suddenly slipped down a driveway and disappeared.

I pulled the Volvo onto the grassy shoulder a few yards from the driveway—a pebbly track with sprigs of grass erupting from beneath the stones. Trees hovered over both sides, creating a sheltered, leafy tunnel. I unlatched the car door, got out, and waited to hear the thud of Alex closing his pickup truck's door. Then I crept down the driveway until I could see his house.

A large white rectangle, like a giant sugar cube, sat on a wide lawn, as open and expansive as a small golf course. There were a few tall birch trees, but no shrubs or other plantings. The expanse of grass began at the edge of the house and ended in a precise line where the woods began. I walked slowly toward the house and stood half-hidden behind one of the larger birch trees, craning my neck to get a glimpse through the front window, when Alex popped out from behind a tree.

"Boo!" he shouted.

"Alex, Jesus," I said. "You nearly gave me a heart attack."

He burst into laughter. "Who's the one spying? You'd make a terrible detective," he said. "All I had to do was look at my rearview mirror to see this crazy yellow Volvo weaving around."

He turned toward the house and looked back at me. "Why don't you come inside for a drink? You can take a look at my house for once."

JUST INSIDE THE front door, I paused to admire a glass vase filled with white lilies. It sat atop a marble table beneath a gold-framed mirror mounted on the wall. The ensemble—the spotless beveled surface of the mirror, the dark green marble with its gray and black veins, the fresh, fragrant flowers—didn't shock me so much as disorient me. This couldn't possibly be Alex's home, I thought. After watching him bumble about in our house, I couldn't imagine him in such a simple, elegant environment.

But Alex moved about the hallway with ease, throwing his keys onto the table, where they clinked against the vase.

"So you wanted to see how I live, huh," he said, talking as he walked into his kitchen.

"I'm not sure," I said, hesitating in the hallway. "I just saw you heading home and decided to follow you."

I heard the refrigerator open. "Do you want a drink?" Alex called out. "I'm having a Diet Pepsi. But I've got herbal tea, if you like. That's pretty nice."

From where I stood I could see a corner of the kitchen, with copper-bottomed pots hanging from the ceiling and a magnificent turquoise tile floor. Brightly colored ceramic plates were displayed on top of the cabinets. The kitchen looked pristine and untouched.

"A drink, Emily?" Alex asked again.

"No, thank you," I replied.

"Go on ahead into the living room. Have a seat, make yourself comfortable."

I walked gingerly across an Oriental silk runner, glancing at framed lithographs of birds on the wall.

A large unframed abstract painting hung on another wall. The subject was distinct, autumn leaves at their colorful peak reflected on the surface of a lake. The vibrant reds and oranges burned like tiny fires in the high-ceilinged, white room.

A baby grand piano dominated one end of the room like a black lake. The sofa and armchair were as white as the walls. A glass table in the shape of a lima bean seemed to float just above the wooden floor, like an elevated, frozen puddle. There was little else in the room, except for another glass side table with a single framed photo and a book called *The Tenor's Son* on the seat of the armchair. Luciano Pavarotti stared up from the cover.

"Actually, I bought the tea as an experiment. The boxes look attractive, like they're going to cure you of something, but the tea's terrible," Alex said, emerging from the kitchen, snapping open a cold soda, a bag of corn chips under his arm.

"Did my mother give you that book?" I asked, pointing to *The Tenor's Son*.

Alex shook his head while sipping the soda. "Got it myself. Found it in the Waldenbooks bargain bin for a dollar. Pretty interesting, although I'm not that far into it. I thought it might be a good idea to find out a little bit about the man."

I watched him as he brought the soda back up to his mouth, his lips reaching for the rim of the can. I felt as if I were looking at Alex for the first time. Even his painter's pants were unusually white, blending in with the room.

"Is my fly down or something?" Alex asked, looking down at himself.

"Oh, no, sorry," I replied, blushing, seating myself on the sofa. It was like perching on a massive snowbank.

"So," he began.

"I didn't expect you to live in a place like this," I said.

Alex opened the bag and offered it to me. He slid a chip into his mouth and leaned back in the chair, perching his feet delicately on an ottoman. "I like it like this," he said.

I looked at the photo on the side table, of two young men who looked like thinner, darker versions of Alex, and a woman with a full face and long hair swept up in a sensible bun.

I nodded toward the photo. "Is this your wife?"

Alex nodded without looking at me. "Linda Alice Pappadopolous. And my two boys. They're both married and living in California."

"Your wife looks very nice." I picked up the picture and inspected it closely.

"She was. Linda made a home for us, for over thirty years. I've done my best to keep it up."

"It's a pretty incredible home," I said, putting the photo back on the table.

"She had good taste, my Linda. To this day I can't believe a woman like her married an ordinary Joe like me."

I laughed.

"She was a lady. Educated. She was always trying to better herself, to enrich her life. Played piano like an angel. And you know me. I can tell a Budweiser from a Heineken, but that's about it."

"Where did you meet her?"

Alex slipped another chip into his mouth. "At a church supper. After we had eaten, she played the piano."

He chewed thoughtfully, the crunching sound magnified by the relative emptiness of the huge room. "Actually, I heard her before I saw her. I was sitting there, drinking coffee, and she began playing the piano. It was incredible, like water flowing out and down around me. I'll never forget it."

Alex hummed a jumble of notes.

" 'Water Music' by Debussy," he explained to me after he had finished, eating another chip. "I've got it on CD if you want to hear it."

I smiled and shook my head. "That's O.K. I know the piece."

We sat still for a while, watching the wind blow through the birches outside. For a long time after the divorce, my mother left Pappa's toothbrush and comb beside the sink in her bathroom, as if he were away on a trip. Even the few items Ben left in my dorm room grew iconic as time passed; I didn't touch his underwear or socks until I moved out. Removing them somehow erased the relationship we had had. I wondered if Alex found solace in his wife's home, or if her things were a kind of punishment for him.

"I must say, you did a beautiful job on this house," I told Alex.

"Oh, no, I didn't work on this house. I'm an engineer by trade. I worked at the wire mill over in Georgetown. A friend of Linda's did the renovation. But I had to quit soon after she got sick. I learned a lot watching the work here so I became a carpenter, doing odd jobs to make ends meet. I've always been pretty good with my hands."

"You fell into it."

"Exactly. Linda decorated this house by herself. She worked on it, the carpets, the artwork, for years, night and day. She had money from her mother. And she had a vision for the kind of home she wanted for her family. Even after she got cancer she worked on it. It was never quite perfect enough for her until just before she died. And I've kept it up just as she did."

Alex rested his soda can on his belt buckle, and crossed his feet. His boot soles were worn down at the corners. "Would you like to take a look at my yard? I was thinking for your mother, it might be nice for her to fix that backyard up a bit."

"I don't know if my mother can afford it," I answered.

"Oh really?"

"Our power's been cut off," I continued. "We can't use the refrigerator or the air conditioner."

Alex sat up, removed his feet from the ottoman, and placed them gently on the ground. "I'm sorry to hear that," he said.

"The money my mother's got, she's got to live on for the rest of her life. And the renovation has been awfully expensive."

Alex paused. "Renovation is expensive. No two ways about it," he said.

"I don't know what we're going to do."

"Would you like to take a break for a while? Would that be the easiest thing?"

"I just wish we hadn't spent as much as we already have," I replied.

"I don't know if I can help you out there," Alex said quietly.

A clock chimed from somewhere deep in the house.

"What bothers me the most is my mother acts so composed about everything, like nothing's wrong," I said.

"I'm sure your mother's fine," Alex replied.

"But she never tells me anything about the money she's got or what she's planning. She's always certain nothing will go wrong, like there's some kind of special immunity to her life. She doesn't think about the future."

From where I sat, five towns north of Pleasant Springs,

with miles of woods and homes between my mother and me, I could clearly picture her at home now, alone, calmly searching through drawers and closets for candles to last her through another night.

Alex laughed dryly. "If you think so much about the future, sometimes you feel like there isn't one. Growing old is a complicated business, Emily. You have to learn to enjoy your life today, to embrace what's within your reach. You're lucky. You're lucky your mother is so good at enjoying herself."

He smiled gently, his elbows resting on his knees, back hunched, his hands hanging before him. "Do you know what it's like to get old?" he asked.

I paused. "What do you mean?"

"To know people who have died. To know your children aren't children anymore. To know you're never going to walk the Great Wall or go to Budapest or become a millionaire.

"Every morning I look in the mirror and half-expect to see the face I had when I was forty. I still feel the same way I did back then, good and strong, but then I see my face. It's a little death every morning, I'm telling you."

Alex crumpled the top of the chip bag closed. "And believe me, a day can be filled with a dozen painful revelations like that," he continued. "That you can't lift something you used to, or hear a sound as clearly, or remember what color your first bicycle was. But then you see a photo of yourself when you were younger, and you can remember so many little things—what the air smelled like, what color the sky was. Even what you were thinking."

Alex lowered his head and was silent, as if lost in one of those photos. "But you learn to let those moments wash over you," he said finally. "It's best to focus on today. You have to live in the moment."

He picked up the soda, finished it with a long, last swig and, after struggling for a moment, crushed the empty can with his hand.

THE NEXT MORNING, Alex arrived early, bringing hot coffee in Styrofoam cups and bagels with lox and cream cheese. "How are you feeling, Hanako?" he asked brightly as soon as he came up the stairs.

My mother, pale and wrapped in a bathrobe, nodded and smiled. "Much better, although I could use some coffee," she said.

Suddenly, the kitchen light blinked on, and the refrigerator's hum filled the room.

"Hey," Alex exclaimed, slapping his hand against his leg, "we're in business."

"How did this happen?" my mother asked. She turned to Alex while opening the lid to a cup of coffee. "Nothing has changed since yesterday."

Alex smiled and shrugged his shoulders. "Let's just say

I've got some friends at the power company." He tore apart a bagel and stuffed a large piece into his mouth, leaving two tiny buds of cream cheese at the corners.

"Why, thank you very much, Alex. You needn't have concerned yourself with my small problems," my mother said, although she was smiling and some color came back into her face.

"Besides, we've got a lot of work to do. Got to get that bathroom done before Pavarotti comes around."

"Yes, yes," my mother replied, looking up at him. "Thank you, Alex."

Alex took a huge gulp of coffee. "Do you want siphonic flush?" he asked.

"'Symphonic flush'?" my mother said.

Alex laughed, wiping his mouth with a paper napkin. "No, no. Siphonic flush. It's a kind of toilet. It sucks water quietly and quickly down the drain. Much more subtle than a regular flush toilet."

"Sounds modern," my mother said, nodding. "I like the idea of a modern, impressive bathroom."

"We barely have electricity," I reminded her. "Maybe you should be shooting for something closer to a hole in the ground and a wooden barrel to bathe in."

She ignored me, launching into a long discourse about Italian marble tubs, like the ones she had seen in her decorating magazine.

"If not Italian marble, then at least cast iron. Or pressed

steel. But no plastic. When I'm taking a bath, I want to feel quality, to have my spirits lifted," she said.

Alex took another bite of his bagel and stuck a hand in his shirt pocket, then patted his back pockets. "Speaking of lifting your spirits, look what I have here," he said, holding up three tickets. "Next Wednesday. Pavarotti at Lincoln Center. What do you say?

My mother clapped her hands. "Oh, Alex! How lovely!"

"A warm-up, Hanako," Alex said. "Before the big day."

INSTEAD OF DRIVING into New York City, my mother insisted on taking the train into Grand Central, the shuttle to Times Square, and then the local uptown subway to Lincoln Center. "You can never predict traffic," she said, declining Alex's offer to take us in his truck. "And the Met closes its doors to people who are late. After all, it isn't a movie theater."

She was happy and talkative for the whole journey into town, pointing out the constellations painted on the ceiling of Grand Central Station while briskly ushering us from the train to the subway. She was proud of her familiarity with the station's underground intricacies, having taken this route countless times, and laughed as she berated me for relying on taxis whenever I visited the city.

As we got off the subway at Sixty-sixth Street, we passed an old man strumming a beat-up electric guitar next to a newspaper kiosk. "Delightful!" she exclaimed, her high voice piercing through the vibrating roar of the subways around us. "This man playing down here, Pavarotti singing up above," she said, dropping a dollar bill into a grimy baseball cap on the ground. "There is music everywhere."

We found our seats high up in the Met's second balcony. From there, the stage seemed strangely small and tilted, as if we were peering down into a puppet theater. People were just beginning to stream in, their footsteps muffled by carpeting, their voices serious and low. I sat by the aisle, with my mother to my left and Alex on her other side.

"Don't you think they look like popcorn balls?" Alex asked, staring up at the large glittering clusters of lights suspended overhead.

"I get excited when they pull them up into the ceiling just before the orchestra starts to play," my mother said, flipping through the program. "You feel something grand is about to begin."

People quietly continued to flow in, until the seats were completely filled. The lights, attached to long poles, began to rise toward the ceiling. Alex watched them go up and looked past my mother, who was sitting forward in her seat, to me. He nodded excitedly. Then the theater slowly darkened and the music began.

I HAD NEVER seen *La traviata* on stage, but knew the music, even some of the libretto, from my mother's repeated record playing at home.

Even in the darkness, I could sense her anticipation, her back not quite touching the chair, her face completely still as light from the stage reflected images of the singers across her glasses.

"'Libiamo, ne' lieti calici,'" she whispered to me, as the music began. "A very important song."

From our seats, I could barely make out the details of Pavarotti's face, although his girth and dramatic gestures were unmistakable from any distance. And while his voice could be heard clearly throughout the opera house, there wasn't anything loud about it. He caressed the audience with his sweet, earnest singing, as if this were the last time he would perform the piece.

I watched my mother listen. While she seemed uncomfortable in her chair—her handbag and jacket a jumble in her lap, her arm awkwardly pressed against her left side because Alex's bony elbow had taken up the armrest—she appeared surreally serene. Her lips slightly parted, the expression on her face fixed. Only her posture changed. When the tenor finished, she broke out into a bout of feverish applause.

"WELL, THAT WAS something," Alex said, standing and clapping as the lights came up. "I really liked that last duet."

"'Parigi, o cara.' I've seen Pavarotti sing it a number of times, but he was especially good tonight." My mother paused before putting on her jacket. "I'll tell him that when I see him next month."

I had momentarily forgotten about Pavarotti's visit. And after seeing him here, in front of a full house, after four standing, stamping ovations, after the shouted bravos and cheers, it felt more unlikely than ever that he was going to show up at our house.

As we filed out of the theater, I grabbed Alex's arm. "Hey, I've got an idea. Do you think we could get my mother backstage to see Pavarotti?"

"What do you mean?"

"You know, see if we can go backstage. Even if it's only for a few seconds, so my mother can see Pavarotti, just to touch base."

Alex looked doubtful. "I don't know. I'm sure they've got pretty tight security."

"Oh, it's not necessary," my mother said, shaking her head vigorously.

Alex looked down at her with an uncertain smile. "I suppose it can't hurt to try. Wait for me by the exits. I'll see what I can do."

He hurried down the aisle toward the empty orchestra pit.

"This is exciting!" my mother said, poking in her handbag as we walked out the door. "If I had known, I would have worn something a bit more formal." She fished out a hand mirror and checked her teeth. "I hope he doesn't think I underdress when I come to the opera," she added.

Ten minutes later, Alex returned, walking slowly up the inclined walkway, shoulders slumped. "Doesn't look good. There's a list with the names of people who are allowed backstage, and you're not on it," he told my mother gently.

My mother straightened up, and held her handbag across her chest. "Not to worry. It'll be fine. No need for anything more than that. Shall we go?"

"Why don't we leave a note with someone?" Alex said. We looked at each other. "Sure," I said.

"But we don't have any paper," my mother countered. We checked our pockets and handbags for something to write on. Alex produced an invoice from a hardware store, I offered my program, my mother had nothing.

"Do you think perhaps we should get some proper paper?" my mother asked. "Not that we should go to much trouble, but if this is going to be delivered to Pavarotti . . ." Her voice trailed off.

Alex glanced at me, the corners of his mouth tightening to suppress a smile or a frown, I wasn't sure. My mother led us to the gift shop, where after much examination, she selected a card with a Klimt painting on the front. Alex wrote the note as my mother dictated, drafting it once on his hardware invoice before copying it onto the card. And before handing it over to a bald man at the theater entrance, Alex waved the card at my mother and kissed it.

We stood outside the Met for a while, watching the fountain in the front. My mother looked triumphant in the moonlight. As the water leapt in the night air, I thought about Pavarotti, entertaining friends in his dressing room or at some restaurant nearby, oblivious to the three of us out here, and wondered why my mother was so confident.

EIGHT

Dietrich Fischer-Dieskau's voice echoed through the bathroom as Alex, on his hands and knees, laid down wide squares of vinyl on the floor. He relished the task, taking his time, as it would be the last thing he needed to do on the house. He hummed along with the baritone, who, as Don Giovanni, was looking forward to a night of romantic conquests. The tape recording sounded slightly warped at times, because, I suspected, my mother had played it often while taking steamy baths.

"Do you know the story of Don Giovanni?" Alex asked me as I cleared out the linen closet, picking out the dingy, old towels from the usable ones, separating the adult sheets and pillowcases from those decorated with bananas in pajamas and sleepy choo-choo trains.

"He was a notorious womanizer," I said, reaching over to the tape player and turning down the volume. "He had affairs with something like a thousand women and left them all, or so the story goes."

"Oh yeah?"

"But in the end, the women get their revenge. Don Giovanni goes up in flames, which, I think, means he's headed for hell."

Alex carefully cut the vinyl around the base of the toilet. He patted the underside of the bowl. "I got a good deal on this," he said. "Not 'symphonic,' as your mother would say. But I figured regular flush toilets have been working all right for years, so no need to spend more money."

"What about that?" I asked, pointing at the glistening lime-green tub.

Alex chuckled. "I told your mother that a marble tub would be too cold and impersonal, kind of like bathing in a fountain in a park. I convinced her to go with a bright, cheerful color, to add some sparkle to the bathroom. So, in the end, we got a fiberglass tub. Looks good, don't you think?"

"You installed that yourself?" I asked. "That's pretty difficult, isn't it?"

Alex nodded. "I was hoping you'd be impressed," he said, smiling.

A soprano launched into "Ah, fuggi il traditor."

THE NEXT MORNING, I tried to fit the small metal strainer filled with finely powdered coffee into the socket on the espresso machine, holding the contraption down with one hand as it skittered on the counter. What happened to the old reliable percolator, I wondered. My mother had also purchased an electric pasta maker and a gelato machine. The filter finally snapped into place, sending a spray of coffee over my arm. I turned on the machine, half-expecting it to explode, and went to retrieve the paper from the front stoop. It was early, the blue sky still streaked with the watery pink tones of dawn. I always enjoyed the fragile light at this particular time, precariously balanced between dawn's rosy gray and the clarity of day.

The living room's new, pale oak floor illuminated the room, opening up the space that had earlier been confined by blue carpeting. The floor had been a near disaster. At first, Alex pulled up the carpet to inspect the old floor and declared it fit enough to refinish. After scrubbing it for a few hours, he hopped into his truck and returned with a sander, a contraption that looked like a cross between a lawn mower and a giant vacuum cleaner.

By early afternoon, he was standing behind the roaring machine as it skimmed across the boards, leaving alarming semicircular scratches in its path. Next, the sander spewed copious clouds of wood dust into the air when Alex didn't realize its collecting bag was full. Before I could complain, he turned the machine off and smoothed his hair back tightly with both his hands as if trying to glue the strands to his head. Then he went into the kitchen to make a phone call.

An hour or so later, a few silent young men, bearded and wearing T-shirts and jeans, trudged in through our front door, each mumbling a quiet but polite hello to my mother. The subcontractors went to work quickly and efficiently, moving with the businesslike energy of an emergency medical team. Alex stood next to me, watching them, shifting his weight from foot to foot. "Getting old, I guess," he said lightly but a bit sadly, relief loosening the lines of his face.

I sipped the beige froth (my mother insisted on calling it *crema*) from the top of my espresso. The coffee was good, but for all the effort, the machine had only dribbled out three-quarters of a cup. I opened the newspaper and skimmed some of the less important foreign headlines.

A Japanese rock star hanged himself from a lamppost with a towel, prompting several young girls in Japan to do the same. The Chinese were drinking French wine, but mixing it with Sprite. Due to cold weather and a diet of dull open-faced sandwiches, Scandinavians were chronically, desperately depressed.

I stopped reading and looked around the room. As much as I disliked it at times, there was an integrity to my mother's house, an appropriateness to its structure, size, shape, and floor plan. Homes that have been lived in for a while have an intangible character that goes beyond aesthetics, a somehow organic quality that reflects the personality of their occupants. My mother was right about not wanting to rid her house completely of its history. Sitting on her sofa, in the freshly finished living room, I felt as settled as I did sitting in her quiet presence.

But there was still something wrong. My mother's house, situated beautifully atop a hill facing west, was bathed each day with light: the kitchen and dining room illuminated in the morning, the living room in the afternoon. Yet, the living room remained dark late into the day, and the light that did enter in the morning came through the opening in the wall separating the living room from the dining room. I had always thought the claustrophobic feel of the living room was due to the carpeting and many books and magazines crowding the tables. But now I could see the problem was with the wall. Alex had installed a row of French doors in the dining room overlooking the backyard, but the dividing wall separating the dining room from the living room cropped the view. I got up and tapped the wall, which sounded light and hollow. It was probably just some gypsum board and studs.

"You're up early," my mother said, coming down the stairs. She was dressed in a blazingly bright sunflower-yellow sweatsuit.

"I went to bed early," I replied.

"It looks to be a beautiful day," my mother remarked, glancing out the window.

"Mom, how would you feel about tearing down the wall between the living room and the dining room?" I asked.

"What?"

"We never use the dining room—everyone eats in the kitchen. So it's sort of silly to have two relatively small rooms when we could have one large space."

The dining room table was piled high with junk mail, old Christmas cards, and unused dishes. After years of neglect, the room had slowly turned into a dusty storage space.

After a long silence, my mother smiled. "I always knew you had a good eye, Emily," she said, patting me on the arm.

"Now, we can't go around knocking down whatever we want," Alex said, laughing later that afternoon. "We don't want ceilings collapsing."

"I'm sure the wall isn't load-bearing. It's just a partition, a divider," I said.

"Even partitions can be load-bearing, Emily."

"Maybe there's an I-beam running the length of the ceiling for support. Or we could extend the lintel," I said. "Why don't you drill into the ceiling and check?"

"Well, all right," Alex said reluctantly. He looked up at

me. "How do you know so much about this stuff, any-way?" he asked.

Alex climbed a ladder, holding his drill, and much to his surprise, and my satisfaction, he quickly hit steel. Soon afterward, he whacked at the wall with a sledgehammer and crowbarred up the studs until all that remained was a mound of rubble. Even before he was finished, I could see my instincts were right, as if the wall had been blocking a current. Light now flowed through the rooms, traveling freely from the front window straight to the French doors that overlooked the backyard. In this new environment, the Danish Modern dining room table and chairs looked like sculpture.

THE DAY OF Pavarotti's concert arrived, but my mother didn't seem at all worried that there was no formal plan to meet the famous tenor. Aside from the call regard-ing her complimentary ticket, no one had contacted her. Yet, with each passing minute my mother's happiness, and her singing, became increasingly frenetic. The bathroom and living room, although still sparsely furnished, were completed, glistening with confidence.

"*Ah! chi mi dice mai, quel barbaro dov'è, che per mio scorno amai, che mi mancò di fé?*" she sang as we descended the stairs into the damp, cool basement.

"So how is this going to work?" I asked.

"*Ah se ritrovo l'empio, e a me non torna ancor,*" she continued, her arms full of sheets. She opened the washer and stuffed the laundry inside, pausing for a moment as I added my towels to the load.

"Donna Elvira's aria, *Don Giovanni*, act one, scene five," she told me, closing the lid and meticulously turning the dials on the washer as if opening a bank vault. "Poor woman."

"Mom, did you hear me?"

"How is what going to work?" she asked, swatting at a loose cobweb that hung from the ceiling.

"Meeting Luciano. Aren't you worried that nothing's been set up?"

"I have my ticket."

"But how are you going to meet him, how do you think you're going to get him here?"

"Sometimes things just happen. You have to have faith." My mother bent over and opened the dryer, picking out a large wad of lint from the filter. "In *La traviata*, Alfredo returns to Violetta before she dies, realizing he had made a mistake, thinking she had cheated on him. And in *L'elisir d'amore*, Nemorino does get the woman he wants in the end, even without the elixir, which is fake anyway. Everything always turns out all right."

My mother believed that good always balanced bad, that life was never overly weighted with one or the other. She'd cite examples of people we knew—my father's painful childhood banished by professional success, Mrs.

Murata's infertility mitigated by her wealth. Virtue was always rewarded, she reasoned; her difficult years were bound to fetch her some form of happiness.

But I had seen enough opera to know that lots of sopranos end badly for all their pain: Lucia di Lammermoor forced to marry a man she doesn't love and driven mad by the man she does; Aida doomed to die in a sealed tomb; and Gilda, whose death is an unfortunate side effect of vengeance gone awry. I saw no moral to be learned from these tales. Some people just had bad luck.

"Life isn't an opera, Mom," I said.

My mother closed the dryer, put the lint in her pocket, and, avoiding my gaze, scanned the rest of the basement behind me. "I decided that this will be my music room," she said quickly. "I'll put a piano down here. The acoustics are excellent."

The basement's cinder-block walls were covered with clumpy dust. The little light that seeped in through the dirt-encrusted windows made the room feel small and made me feel claustrophobic.

"I'm worried about the foundation," I said, looking at the concrete floor, softened and stained with the water that appeared after heavy rains.

"Oh, Alex says he can fix that—he's going to dig out around the outside and seal the walls. He says we can put in a raised floor. Dehumidifiers will take care of the rest.

But, first of all, I'm going to get rid of all these old things," my mother said.

A miniature train track wove through the room atop a series of wooden tables built by my father. The tables were painted green, and tiny, frosted trees, toy buildings, and plastic people still dotted their surfaces. There was a boy raking invisible leaves, a man carrying a briefcase, a woman walking a tiny brown dog. There were no trains, however. Pappa left behind nearly all his belongings—his clothes, his books, his photos, even his academic awards —but he had come back for his trains.

"I never understood his fascination with these things," my mother said. But it occurred to me that these tiny trains, humming through a picture-perfect neighborhood, were my father's version of the stately homes and mani-cured lawns that so fascinated my mother.

I looked at her. "So, what time's the concert?" I asked.

"Eight o'clock," my mother said firmly. "Will you be home around eleven? I want you to meet him."

I smiled. "Sure."

"It will happen," she said. "The house is ready. I am ready. It will happen."

As I drove to work, the young, gray evening set-tling behind the trees, I felt a deep sense of dread.

I imagined how my mother envisioned her life: The

stage is set with a dreamy backdrop of green hills against a darkening pink sky. A young girl sits on a bench with her older brother. They are both singing, their untrained voices accompanied only by the distant sound of waves lapping the shore.

Scene Two: The girl, now a beautiful young woman, is wooed by a stranger. They sing a tender love duet and he whisks her off to the United States. The backdrop changes to rolling suburban neighborhoods, huge, cavernous supermarkets, and, finally, to the interior of a Western home, dominated by the blue carpet of our living room. For the scene in which the woman discovers her husband's infidelity, a starkly barren bedroom. The curtain comes down as the woman sits at the kitchen table, alone, her head in her hands, the backdrop painted with the big yellow flowers of our kitchen wallpaper.

Act Two: The character of the contractor enters, his gravelly baritone filling the house as he sings and works. The backdrops change, showing a series of renovated rooms. The act closes with a triumphant duet between the woman and contractor, sung in front of the fountain at Lincoln Center.

The third act begins with an aria, sung by the woman in the parking lot of a university. She expresses dismay at love lost, but sings thanks to her contractor for helping rebuild her life. She goes into the theater and finds her seat, front row center. Pavarotti comes on stage and begins to sing. When he pauses, the woman sings back from her seat, the superior quality of her voice shocking the tenor on stage. He sings again while extending a hand toward the mysterious woman, who joins him on stage. The opera ends with the conclusion of the duet, the two singers enjoying thunderous applause.

I sighed, swerving to avoid hitting a dead squirrel. At least my mother could legitimately sing the praises of Alex. After all my misgivings about him, the renovation was completed on time. And besides treating us to the opera, he had agreed to extend her credit on some of the work and had renovated the bathroom for free. "Wasn't that kind?" she said to me. "Wasn't I right?"

THE CASHIER TWIRLED her long hair around her fingers and picked at the split ends. Across the room, chef caps bobbed and dipped like the beaks of exotic birds. I watched Hiro throw a green pepper from behind his back so that it sailed over his shoulder, but he missed catching it. He tried the same thing twice more, missing both times. His tableful of guests gasped when he grabbed a knife from his holster, and tossed it in the same manner. But he caught it, as he did each time. The diners burst into relieved applause.

The room hummed with conversation, punctuated by the sound of metal scraping against metal and occasional bursts of staccato chopping. Waitresses in taut kimonos cut through the air thick with cigarette smoke and smoke from the grills. I retrieved my tray from the wait station near the bar and went to table eight, one of three tables assigned to me for the evening. Seated around the dull steely surface of the grill were six thuggish men, all sporting versions of the same cruel haircut: shaved at the sides, long in the back, and the tops seemingly permed. Their leader, tight and sinewy as a wrung towel, jerked his head from left to right like a boxer while his knees bobbed with restless energy.

Each man ordered two entrees, and Hiro worked furiously at the grill. Back in the kitchen, Tetsu was in a dismal mood, having cut himself early in the shift. He walked around with his arms at his sides, occasionally stopping to inspect a thick gauze bandage wrapped around his index finger.

"Does it hurt?" I asked, pulling bowls of salad from the refrigerator. I ladled dressing out of a stainless steel cauldron, slopping a little over each bowl.

Tetsu shook his head. "No pain. I just feel bad for the rest of the chefs. Especially Hiro. He'll end up doing all my work."

Hiro banged his cart through the swinging door, accompanied by a burst of laughter from the dining room. Stacks of empty metal platters teetered in front of him, his chef's cap slightly askew. He left the empty cart and switched to Tetsu's fully loaded one, heading back to the dining room without even looking up at us. I followed him out and went to the bar. Roberto, the Filipino bartender, announced that we were out of melon liqueur.

"No Green Buddhas, no Balmy Sea Breezes, no Far East Fruit Fantasies," he said.

"Got it," I replied. As I watched him speak, I realized I had never seen Roberto's legs.

"Push Blue Skies over Fuji. We've got plenty of curaçao."

I walked to the dining area and saw Hiro bow to his new guests. At the adjoining table, the boxer and his friends were shoveling forkfuls of food into their mouths, their chopsticks stuck like TV antennae into the bowls of rice.

Hiro turned and caught my eye while pouring a stream of oil from a decanter onto the grill.

"Shrimp," he mouthed with raised eyebrows. I hesitated and he tipped his head toward the kitchen.

I nodded, but as I was heading out, the boxer motioned to me. "I want a Geisha Kiss," he said, wiping his mouth with the back of his hand.

As I turned again toward the kitchen Mariko came through the swinging doors. She smiled wanly. "Table six is getting restless."

I glanced back at the table. Seated were plump twin boys dressed in similarly floppy dungarees, a tanned, well-to-do couple wearing identical white golf shirts, and an elderly man drumming his fingers on the tabletop beside his nurse. I picked up menus and hurried to them. "This is a fun place," the old guy said.

They ordered drinks and I headed back toward the bar. As I passed Hiro, he shot me a concerned look while digging metal spatulas into the sliced onion and zucchini cooking on the grill. "Shrimp," he hissed, tossing the vegetables high in the air.

The bar area was already congested with fresh drinks and empty, dirty glasses. Roberto sighed dramatically as I searched for a spot to put my order slips, resorting to the wet side of a cold bottle of beer. I rushed through the swinging doors to the kitchen and opened the walk-in refrigerator.

"What are you doing?" Mariko asked, pouring boiling water into a tea kettle.

"Hiro forgot the shrimp," I replied.

"Oh, no, he's made a mistake. One of his customers is allergic to shrimp. I removed it from his cart."

"Really? He's asked me a few times to get it."

"Remind him. He's made a mistake."

I swung back to the bar to pick up the boxer's order. Gin and tonics, beer, and Cokes crowded the counter. I spotted the drinks for table six, but nothing resembling a Geisha Kiss.

"Roberto, did you get my other order?" I asked, loading my tray with drinks.

"For what?"

"A Geisha Kiss."

"A what?"

"A Geisha Kiss."

"We don't have anything like that."

"Are you sure?"

Roberto laughed, popping a maraschino cherry into his mouth.

I tucked the order pad into my obi and met the gaze of the boxer from across the room. He smiled, his body still twitching.

"Where is the shrimp?" Hiro asked, his voice directly behind my neck. When I turned, he looked up my nose.

"I've already done the steak. Everything is going backwards."

"Oh, Hiro. Mariko told me someone at your table is allergic to shrimp, so you're not supposed to cook it."

Hiro snorted. "Mariko!" He paused for a moment, his eyes distracted, and then hurried back to his grill. The obese twins were getting restless, strain showing on the tanned parents' faces. The boxer continued to grin at me, and I could see a large family being seated at my third table. I patted my obi and pulled out my order pad with table six's dinner orders still on it.

"Sometimes I hate this work," I said to Mariko when she appeared at my side.

"Work is work," she replied.

"My rhythm's all messed up. I haven't cleared my first table, and the second one hasn't got soup, and I haven't given their dinner orders to any chef yet. And now I've got a new table."

Mariko smiled, looking as serene as a lily pond. "Don't worry," she said. "I'll take care of it."

And she did. I watched her take drink orders and food orders at the same time, and then bring out bowls of salad balanced along her arms. She distributed the drinks carefully, holding back her kimono sleeve so as not to drag it across the grill. And with rubber bands and paper, she even transformed chopsticks into wooden tweezers for the twins.

I POURED MYSELF a glass of water and stood in the kitchen, thinking of the concert. Maybe it would all work out; somehow, my mother would be able to slip backstage to see the star. He would pass up postconcert celebrations to follow an overly excited Japanese woman into a beat-up Volvo and drive deep into the suburban night until they reached her house, clean and tranquil atop a hill: a renovated temple.

Or maybe if he doesn't show up, the things that irritated me the most about my mother—her disorganized life, her astonishing, sometimes baseless faith, her bottomless passion for opera—would sustain her.

"Your table is seated," Mariko called to me as she entered the kitchen. I tucked an order pad into my obi and headed slowly out. "Europeans," she added.

Hiro sighed and began tying a clean yellow kerchief around his neck, while Tetsu prepared his next cart. "Europeans always want to change the flavor of the food," he said. "'Oh, that is too much soy sauce. Please, do you have more ginger? More oil? More green onion?' So picky." He yanked the ends into a tight knot. "Makes me mad."

There were ten people waiting, two more than the table was designed to hold, meaning two more bowls of rice and salad than the trays could accommodate. Even from across the room, I could see the table was particularly noisy, a well-dressed bevy of joking, jovial friends. As I approached, I penetrated an aura of cologne. A large man sat in the middle, the center of attention.

I patted my obi, feeling for a pen, but looked up when I heard the voice. It rose above the din and clatter of the grills, past the mournful plucking of taped koto music, filling the high, empty space to the ceiling.

"*Una furtiva lagrima negl'occhi suoi spuntò*," the voice sang, "*quelle festose giovani invidiar sembrò: che più cercando io vo?*"

The steakhouse became eerily still. Twenty feet away, Mariko's hand froze in midair, a salad bowl cradled in her fingers; the only sound was meat sizzling on a grill. I had heard the voice a million times on our old record player. I had heard the voice just last month. It was Pavarotti.

"Bravo!" someone yelled. Tables broke out in applause. Pavarotti half-stood and bowed, sending the flowing end of a white silk scarf over his shoulder with a dramatic swat. The mouth I had known as a big black O on record covers was in front of me, smirking, coughing, laughing. His heavy beard and mustache covered his cheeks and chin like a rough wool overcoat. "I am in terrible voice tonight," he said with a frown to no one in particular.

"Oh no, on the contrary," said a woman sitting across from him. She shook her head emphatically, her long, sparkly earrings batting the sides of her face. "You're magnificent," she cooed.

"Oh, please," Pavarotti murmured, lowering his eyes. He exaggerated his expressions, as if trying to convey his feelings to the back of the room. Modesty meant pulling out his lower lip and gazing at his hands.

Then he smiled, his heavily lidded eyes half open, and continued the conversation momentarily interrupted. "Nemorino knows that Adina finally loves him when he spots *'una furtiva lagrima'* in her eye. A furtive tear. And Adina, despite having turned him away earlier because she felt fidelity was impossible, wants Nemorino's love and wins him back. Not with any magical elixir, but with her smile and eyes." He snickered. "I wonder how long that relationship would have lasted."

"Oooo," the woman with the earrings murmured.

"What are you doing here?" I asked. He looked up at

me, his eyes shimmering and clear like coffee, his mouth gigantic. "You're supposed to be performing at Purchase," I told him.

"Are you my waitress?" he asked. I nodded.

"You sound more like my dear mother, but she's not as pretty as you," he said, giving me a sly smile. The table tittered and followed his lead when he opened the menu. A thick gold ring with a red stone twinkled on his pinky.

"I saw you last month at the Met," I said, clicking my pen uncontrollably, my eyes struggling to focus on Pavarotti's considerable face. "My mother thought you sang 'Parigi, o cara' really well."

Pavarotti raised his eyebrows and smiled.

"But why aren't you performing?" I asked. "At Purchase? Tonight?" I had difficulty getting enough air into my lungs to complete my sentences with one breath; as Pavarotti's table grew quiet I felt my obi tighten so that I soon wouldn't be able to speak.

Pavarotti's forehead wrinkled into three horizontal lines. He turned to his tablemates to shrug and lift his hands in bafflement. He then burst out laughing, and his entourage joined in on the joke, a chortling mass of purple and blue cashmere, gold watches, and expensively styled hair.

One of the men at the table spoke for him: "His doctor tells him he has bronchial allergies. Singing under these conditions would be irresponsible." Pavarotti sniffed. "Irresponsible," his friend repeated, looking at me meaning-fully. "Everyone always makes such a fuss."

"He was supposed to be coming to my mother's house," I continued, my voice ringing high and unreal in my ears.

Pavarotti folded his arms on the wooden bit of table that framed the grill and smiled gently. "Darling," he said, his tongue rolling, then releasing the *r*. "I have fans every-where. From Tulsa to Thailand, even Tibet." The other man took over. "It would be impossible for him to visit all of them in their homes."

"But he told my mother he would. At the Met . . .

Pavarotti shook his head and threw his hands in the air.

My eyes searched for some kind of recognition in his face, some sign that he recalled my mother's happiness for those ten minutes in his dressing room. His face remained blank, crossed by a ripple of irritation. But then he took my hand. "Is your mother Asian, about five feet tall?" he asked.

"You remember her?" I said.

He looked at me, his lips pursed with concern, his fin-gers closing warmly around mine, and I started to believe him. He remembered.

Then a man screamed. I looked up toward a flash of light and saw a tower of flame disappear in the air. The old man at table six flailed his arms, and I could see Hiro's yel-low hat standing still above a crowd of craning diners. Mariko dashed from the kitchen with a wet towel in her hand and held it to the old man's head. When she removed it, the man's white hair was singed black in front, his eyebrows nearly gone. Burnt shrimp sputtered on the grill.

The guests sat back down uneasily in their chairs, leaving Hiro standing, alone. He bowed deeply and then walked quickly toward the front door. "Baka yaro," he mumbled, tossing his yellow chef's cap onto the floor.

The corners of Pavarotti's mouth twitched, as if in spasm, and he released my hand. The surrounding air hit my fingers with a distant coolness.

"Hiro!" Mariko called out, running after him through the front door. I ran after him as well. His head looked small and vulnerable, unprotected by his chef's cap, and I noticed he was balding.

"It's not a disaster," Mariko said as we reached the parking lot behind him.

He hurried toward his Pinto with an uneven gait, untying his apron and kerchief and flinging them behind him. Opening the creaky door, he slid into the driver's seat and slammed the door so hard the entire car shook. He started the engine with a full-throttle whine and took off, his tires screaming and burning black onto the pavement. Mariko and I were left behind in a blast of blue exhaust.

Mariko, hands on her hips, shook her head. We watched his yellow car pause at the bottom of the restaurant's driveway, turn south, then zoom away.

"Where is he going?" I asked.

"Florida," she replied.

"Florida?"

Mariko nodded. "He's always had a fantasy about Florida, driving along Daytona Beach, learning to surf, eating oranges off the tree. There's a steakhouse down there somewhere, too."

"What makes you think he's decided to go now?" I asked.

"Gil," she said. "And the Harley-Davidson Gil never rode. Hiro doesn't want to be dead before he lives his life."

We stood in the parking lot for a few moments, moths batting against the lights high above us. Then the front door swung open, and Pavarotti and his entourage streamed out onto the front steps. We watched in silence as the group headed for two Mercedes-Benzes parked at the far end of the lot.

The car doors closed with muffled thumps and the sedans filed past Mariko and me, as solemnly as a funeral motorcade. I spotted Pavarotti sitting in the backseat of the second Mercedes, his hands gesturing wildly.

THE CROWDS USUALLY began to thin at around nine-thirty, but tonight they continued to pour in, filling up the bar and blocking the hallway that the waitresses used. "On your right! On your right!" Mariko called out as she burst out of the pantry, carrying two trays. The cigarette smoke from the bar floated toward the dining room, mingling with the heavy smoke from the grills. As I headed down the hallway toward the pantry, my tray loaded with empty dishes, the smoke stung my eyes, the waiting customers looking like laughing, talking blurs.

Mariko had picked up Hiro's yellow cap from the floor and put it on the front counter in the pantry. I looked closely at it, a sheath of cotton crisply starched and ironed. Hiro had spent so many hours wearing this thing, working in front of hot grills and entertaining guests, that I almost expected it to have absorbed some of his ebullience, some of his personality. But without him, it was just part of a discarded uniform.

At ten-thirty, I scraped the last of the ginger-carrot dressing onto a bowl of salad. The five other bowls remained undressed. I stared at the empty stainless steel cauldron, its inside coated with orange-tinted oil. I had never seen it empty.

"What should we do?" I asked Tetsu, who peeked into the cauldron from over my shoulder.

"Hiro's the only one who knows the recipe," he said. "He kept it a secret for ten years."

Customers often asked me how the dressing was made, or if the ingredients were available in the U.S. When I'd repeated these questions to Hiro, he had replied with a shrug that company policy was to ignore the requests. But I suspected that he planted stories in the minds of the customers. As a result, the dressing grew shrouded in culinary mystery: The orange color was rumored to come from a rare ginger grown only in southern Japan; there was talk that the recipe had been uttered from the lips of a dying chef, the last of a line of chefs to cook for the Emperor. One night, a diner told me that he had heard that the dressing could cure his arthritis.

I'd had no idea that Hiro had created the dressing. Despite his callousness, his complaints about the drudgery of his job, he cared enough to leave his imprint, to help shape the steakhouse, to create a bit of his own history.

I examined the many decanters lined up on a shelf and poured all of the oil from one into the cauldron. My mother could improvise fiercely and with confidence, reaching into a cupboard for jars of dried herbs, bending over the stove to taste from the pots in front of her, adding a pinch of this or a drop of that, moving like a conductor at the podium, directing an orchestra.

"Get all the lemons you can find," I told Tetsu.

"Lemonade dressing?" Tetsu asked.

While he rummaged around the refrigerator, I rushed to the bar, took all the lemons, and returned to the kitchen. We cut the lemons in half and squeezed the juice into the oil in the cauldron, the pungent tang scenting the air. I added chopped garlic, salt and pepper, and a few spoonfuls of sugar.

"Taste it," I told Tetsu.

He dipped a finger into the dressing and stuck it in his mouth.

"Sour," he said, lips puckered, "but tastes good. It'll cut through the grease."

I stirred the dressing with a ladle and spooned it over the rest of the salads and returned the cauldron to the refrigerator.

Just as I was leaving, Mariko flew into the pantry, her normally cool complexion glistening.

"You've got a phone call, Emily," she said, yanking open the refrigerator and lugging out the dressing. "He's on hold, line eight."

"Who is it?" I asked.

"I don't know."

I bolted out the door, and the smoke and din of the crowd hit me like a blast of exhaust from the back of a bus. I pushed through the throng to the bar, picked up the phone, and pressed line eight.

"Hello?"

I heard a man's voice, but couldn't make out any words through the din of people talking at the bar and the connection's crackly static.

"Hello?" I repeated. Suddenly, I thought it might be Pavarotti, calling to apologize. The man spoke again.

"Mr. Pavarotti?" I said, pressing my hand over my free ear.

"Hello? Can you hear me?" the man said faintly. The voice was too deep to be Pavarotti's.

"Alex?" I asked.

"Emily? It's Ben. Sounds like I'm catching you at a bad time."

"Ben?"

"I got your work number from your mother. I hope you don't mind."

"Aren't you supposed to be in Vietnam?"

"I just got back."

"You sound like you're calling from a tunnel," I shouted above a woman's laughter. Someone stepped on my foot and I stifled a cry.

"I'm on a cell phone. I'm driving to New York. Right now I'm on Interstate 80. I figure I'll be in Tarrytown in under an hour."

"You're coming here?"

"I was wondering if you're free for a drink tonight."

"Tonight?" The area around the bar started to clear. "You want to see me?'

"Yeah. I can pick you up, if you like."

"You wouldn't believe the night I've had."

"A rough crowd?"

"Sort of." I paused for a moment, and was suddenly flooded with thoughts of our last days together. "But what about Beijing University?" I asked.

"I'm still going to Beijing, but not as a student. I've got a job. I'll tell you about it later."

"Oh."

A frisson of static rippled across the line.

"Listen, I've got something I've got to do tonight. But can we go out later this week? I'm glad you called." I watched the doors swing open and yet another noisy party of ten walk in. "I'm not working this Saturday," I added.

"Saturday, sure. I'll call you."

"O.K."

"I brought you back something from Vietnam. A pound of very special coffee. See you."

I hung up the phone and turned to meet Roberto's interested gaze. "You look like you've just been crowned Miss America," he said, working a toothpick through his lower teeth.

I returned to the pantry to retrieve my tray, but my elation deflated as soon as I entered the dining room. The chefs were frenzied, some tending two tables at a time, cooking with a trancelike concentration. A layer of smoke hovered above the diners' heads. From the sound of the voices and laughter, some of them were obviously drunk.

It wasn't until one-thirty in the morning that Mariko lugged the large wooden tip box to the kitchen table. Though each waitress stuffed their tips into a different slot, the money was distributed evenly to all the staff. She lifted the lid. The box was overflowing with cash. She looked at the money for a moment before pulling out and smoothing open a few crumpled bills.

"God, I'm exhausted," I said, looking over Mariko's shoulder.

"You worked very well tonight," Mariko told me. "Look at the tips."

I yawned.

We counted the money in silence for a while, Mariko going through the smaller bills while I fished through the tip box for quarters and stacked them in groups of four.

"You know, there are a lot of things that Hiro used to do besides just cooking," Mariko said.

"Really? Like what?"

"He had managerial responsibilities. Ordering the food, hiring staff, planning work schedules, promotion and advertising. You should think about whether you're interested in taking his place."

"Me?" I looked at Mariko. "You want me to do that?"

She laughed. "Don't act so shocked. You work hard, you get along with people, you have energy. And didn't you study accounting in college? Why wouldn't we want you?"

I thought about Hiro hurtling down the highway toward Florida, or wherever he was going, his white shirt finally unbuttoned at the neck, free from the tight grip of his yellow kerchief.

After changing into my clothes, I sat for a while in the empty locker room. The other waitresses were already upstairs, collecting their share of the tips. Soon, the chefs would return from a cigarette break by the rock garden and make dinner for the staff in the kitchen. Even with the nightly intrusion of outsiders, there was a comfortable predictability to the steakhouse, a routine that varied little from day to day, down to this after-hours meal: drinks, soup, salad, meat, rice, ice cream, tea. Each ritual slid precisely into the next, like the many planks of wood that made up the steakhouse.

I carefully folded my two-piece kimono and rolled up the tabi as Mariko always did for me. I lay them in my cubbyhole, lined up my plastic zori next to them, and curled my obi around everything. My flowered uniform still looked surprisingly fresh, even after all those summers, the pinks and reds girlishly bright.

I walked out into the hallway and looked at the time clock. 2:02 A.M. I punched out, and left.

THE DOUBLE YELLOW line shimmied beneath me like a snake as I drove home. Perhaps Hiro was still driving, too, heading down to Florida, the air slowly becoming warmer and balmier, the vegetation lusher and greener, his mood lighter. As he hurtled south, I thought of us both on the road, two points moving further and further away from each other.

The cool, damp evening buffeted the side of my face. I thought about the farmer in Hokkaido who had built a home for his family, never imagining that it would one day become a restaurant, transplanted from rice paddies to a quarter acre of grass facing a parkway. It would have been as unlikely a possibility for him as my mother's house in Pleasant Springs being taken apart, moved to Turkey, and reconstructed as a modern American café, serving up burgers and fries to diners admiring the quaint suburban details. An identity cannot be changed so abruptly without the loss of a soul.

Maybe finding one's true self is like building a house and then making it a home. The thought of studying architecture still frightened me, but now it was also exhilarating. I wasn't sure I'd be able to keep from falling, but I knew I'd eventually make it to level ground.

FROM THE END of our street I could see the glare of the lamp from our living room split into straws of yellow light by the trees. I turned into the driveway with a dry mouth, imagining how it had been at Purchase: anxious music students turning away angry ticket holders; my mother's silence while driving home. I imagined her crumpled on the couch in a wrinkled dress, Alex's flawed handiwork surrounding her.

I parked the car in the driveway and walked up a pair of fractured slate steps into the backyard. It was a clear night, the early-morning sky the color of blueberries, the smell of grass mixing with the odor of fried meat that clung to my hair. The ground felt spongy. Pierre's basketball hoop and backboard, still attached to a steel pole, lay on its side by the house, like something dead.

I crept up the stairs to the back door and looked in the window. I could see through to the living room, past the kitchen stove, where a blue flame glowed beneath a kettle. My mother was sitting on the far end of the sofa, her right foot tucked behind her left ankle, her eyes focused on the floor, her face expressionless. Then she shook her head in the way she used to late at night when talking in the kitchen with Charlotte and me, telling us whether or not she'd return to Japan after the divorce, or debating what to do with the rest of her life.

I raised my hand to open the door. But then my mother's mouth moved, and I strained to hear.

What I heard was a deep baritone.

"*Là ci darem la mano, là mi dirai di sì,*" it sang, distinctly and loudly, although slightly off-key. "*Vedi, non è lontano, partiam, ben mio, da qui.*"

"*Vorrei, e non vorrei, mi trema un poco il cor; felice, è ver, sarei, ma può burlarmi ancor,*" my mother sang back, looking up, her face glowing. Suddenly she burst out laughing. Alex joined in, and they continued to laugh, their voices resounding in the nearly empty room as if they had just moved into a new house, most of their belongings still packed in boxes.